# THE WELSH HERCULES

Snapshots of a Strongman's Life

## G S BLOCKLEY & D J THACKER

Amazon Books

ISBN: 9798442888973

Cover logo by: James Graham, Saloon Signs, Glasgow.

**"You Showmen are a kingdom within a kingdom – guard it well."**

H M The Queen on a visit to King's Lynn Mart, 1953

## INTRODUCTION – S BLOCKLEY

To be honest, I'm surprised no one has written about Jack Lemm before now.

However, the BBC came to Jack's door, in Swansea, when he was in his late 70's, to enquire about doing a documentary on his life. Jack sent them away. He wanted nothing to do with that nonsense.

I hope you enjoy 'Jack's journey'. His life was all about his family and making a living the best way he could. What a very courageous and exciting life he lived - a true grafter with veins of steel. He certainly was my hero as a kid growing up.

It's amazing to me that I've finally got to tell Jack's story. I turned 60 during the writing of this book and it was a very poignant moment for me to realise that this long-held dream was now coming true.

I would like to thank my good friend D. J. Thacker for all his invaluable knowledge and assistance in the making of this book. Also, to everyone who has shared with me their stories and snippets of information and photos during our lengthy research, I would like to say I am truly thankful.

You can let me know your thoughts about my very first venture into book writing in a message on my Facebook page (Steven Blockley) or by following @welsh_hercules on Instagram. All messages will be replied to.

Giovani Lamnea Snr
and
Rovena Lamnea

Jack's parents, with Giovani in his Mercantile
Marine (Merchant Navy) uniform

# Chapter One

## 1905

Frank Owens looked out over the North Dock and swore.

There were too many people. It was getting too popular. Anything with this number of men gathering in one place was sure to attract the police, and that wasn't good for business. He figured there were around a hundred dockers present, some just leaving shifts, some that should be home asleep. There were even a couple who were supposed to be working right then – another red flag to those who might cause him trouble.

If it were just the men, he reflected, he could probably handle it, but it was the hangers-on who were likely to create the biggest problems. The tarts were out in force. Owens' men were in the crowd collecting bets, but as long as men could be swayed towards spending their money on making a petticoat rise, he knew he'd never take as much as he should. North Dock was small and badly lit and, especially since the Prince of Wales dock had been built (and whatever that new one was going to be that was currently under construction), it was largely used as a last resort. That made it the perfect venue for Owens, but it also made it a haven for the town's strumpets. In a way, he reflected, his event was actually stepping on their territory. That was not the case for the Trade Unionists, however. Gathered in a corner of the yard, banners higher than everyone else, they were as likely to cause a riot as win converts. He needed to get things started before someone said the wrong thing.

Owens plunged into the crowd, pushing his way past fellow dockers until he was at the circle in the centre of the yard. After the crush of the mob, stepping into the ring felt like breaking through into another world. It was only a rough shape marked out by packing cases and with sawdust scattered across the cobblestones, but it was the reason they were all there.

The two combatants were waiting for him, each with their crowd of supporters on the other side of the wooden boxes. Both were stripped to the waist, bruises and cuts from previous bouts showing on their bodies. Jim Tanner was closest to him and at 20 years old, the senior fighter by three years. His flabby body had initially led a lot of men to bet against him, but they had soon found out that he was surprisingly fast and his weight could be a weapon rather than a hindrance. His chest and back were covered in tattoos – legend had it that he got a new one for every winning bout. Tanner caught Owens' eye and smiled before spitting on the ground.

Tanner wasn't a local guy. Owens had arranged for him to come across from Bristol where he had garnered a reputation as a vicious fighter. He was the reason for the large turnout – not because people expected him to win, but because an outsider was daring to take on their champion.

His opponent was on the other side of the ring. He was easily a head taller than the Bristolian, but then he was taller than most of the men present. Despite his youth, there was a stillness to him, the eye of the storm. Like Tanner, he was sat on a smaller packing box but his body was lean, muscles showing beneath pale skin with every slight movement. There was power in his frame, coiled and waiting to escape.

Owens nodded to one of his men standing on the side lines and he started to pound on a large metal box with a plank. The crowd fell silent. Standing in the centre of the ring, Owens began his speech.

"Ladies and gentlemen," he shouted, gratified by the slight ripple of laughter that greeted his first word, "Welcome to this evening's entertainment."

There was a cheer from the mob.

"Tonight we will see two equally matched warriors meeting in this hallowed space - Hercules versus Heracles! Zeus versus Jupiter!"

There were a few sarcastic 'ooh's from the crowd and a lone 'Get on with it!' but most here knew Owens' love for Music Hall and they were willing to put up with a bit of showmanship before the main event.

"On my right," Owens continued, "we have Jim Tanner – the Bristol Butcher, the undefeated terror of the Avon!"

Tanner stood up and bowed to the crowd, revelling in the cheers.

"And, worst of all," Owens continued, "an Englishman!"

The cheers turned to boos and laughter. Tanner, caught up in the moment, shook his fists at anyone close by.

"And to my left," Owens shouted, aware that the crowd would quieten for his next words, "our local champion. The strongman of Swansea.

The All-England Cornish Wrestling Champion of 1903. The Welsh warrior – Jack! Lamnea!"

The crowd erupted. Jack stood up and threw his arms wide, flexing his muscles. One of the men behind him passed him a long iron bar. The tall man held it above his head and effortlessly bent it into a V-shape. He tossed it to the ground amidst a fusillade of cheers.

Owens let the crowd die down a bit before continuing.

"Gentlemen," he said, addressing the two men in the ring, "this is a wrestling match. I don't want to see any punching, or biting, or gouging – you're not in a back alley, you're in God's own Swansea!" – another cheer – "and the winner will take away his prize money only if I judge it to have been a fair fight!"

Both men nodded and the crowd quietened again as they took their opening stances.

Owens took a square of cloth out of his pocket and held it above his head.

"Let battle commence!" he yelled. The cloth hit the ground and Owens, never mistaken for a foolish man, got out of the way as fast as he could.

It wasn't a long walk home from the Docks and Jack was certainly not wanting for company.

His body ached from the treatment Tanner had dealt it – the man fought dirty but in the end he'd lost. Most of the men surrounding Jack on his walk had won money because of it. They were happy and, when they got home, their wives would be happy with the little extra going into the savings. At least it meant Jack wouldn't get dark looks from the women in the morning. He just fought - it was their husbands' fault if they lost money on him, but he still got some of the blame if it happened.

A man Jack vaguely recognised as living two streets over from him slapped him on the back as he passed.

"Excellent fight, man!" he called out. Jack smiled and waved back, not showing that the friendly blow had hit him exactly where Tanner had got in a series of close rabbit punches out of sight of Owens. Something had cracked inside him, he was sure. But it would heal.

Besides, when he had Tanner pinned to the ground, face pushed into the cobbles and one hand slapping the stone to submit, it had been worth it.

His prize money helped too, but the real reason he did it was for that moment. Frank Owens had thrown in that line about his Cornish Wrestling title, and it was true, but that was a more formal fight than he'd had here. Rules were just suggestions in a street wrestling match and in all honesty, Jack was prouder of his victory here than at the Championships.

It was turned ten o'clock and a warm Autumn night. More of the well-wishers had peeled off now to go to their homes. The streets were dark but the sound of raucous singing as the men parted could be heard clearly from beyond the houses.

Jack was left with his thoughts. He could see and hear the railway to his right, the clink and rumble of loading stock being moved along the lines, filled with goods brought off the docks. Bound for big cities, for England, maybe even Scotland. Places Jack knew he would never see.

Further off, the night glowed with a fierce heat coming from the Morfa Copperworks. Large groups of chimneys pierced the night sky, some with flames atop them, all pushing out thick acrid smoke. Huge piles of slag glittered darkly in the distance. The Vicar at St John's had, from the comfort of his pulpit, likened the sight of the foundries at night to Hell. He was new to the area – spoke with an English accent – and after the service a few of his parishioners had pulled him aside to explain the error of his description, given that most of his congregation worked, or had family that worked, at the foundries. All the same, Jack could see his point.

He was glad he worked on the Docks. The breeze coming off the Tawe as it made its way to Swansea Bay helped to keep most of the foul-smelling copper smoke away, and it was honest work. As one of the strongest men there, even at age 17, he was in demand. As long as his back held out, he could get any overtime he wanted.

As he turned into Jersey Street and looked down the terraces towards his home, the thought of overtime seemed good. Not because of the money, but because it kept him away from here.

*** 

Jack was a big man, 6ft 4inches in his stocking feet, but something about opening the door to this house always made him feel small. It wasn't having to duck slightly to get in through the door, it wasn't moving around the cramped conditions – those were so common to him now as to be almost unconscious reflexes. It was the people there.

Well, one person.

As he stepped into the living room, his mother looked up at him. She was sat over by the fireplace, even though the grate was empty, softly illuminated by a gas lamp. She smiled as he came in and lifted a finger to her lips. Her eyes darted to the back door.

Jack smiled in return and nodded. He lifted a hand to indicate that he was going upstairs, to the room he shared with his younger brother, but winced in the action as another bruise revealed itself.

His mother started to get up out of concern, but Jack shook his head, waving her back down into her seat. "All's good," he whispered.

His mother still looked concerned but a noise from outside made her focus on a more immediate problem. Before she could look back at Jack, the door from the backyard opened and Jack's father stumbled in from the privvy, fastening the belt on his trousers as he came.

As he saw Jack, he stopped and scowled. There was a moment of silence as the two men looked at each other and then Jack turned to go up the stairs.

"No time for your father, then?" the older man barked at him. He was speaking in Greek, the language the whole family used at home, the language he'd been born into.

Jack considered answering him in Welsh – they could all speak both languages and varying degrees of English, but he knew that his father hated hearing anything but his mother tongue in the house. 'It's a family thing' he would say. 'Heritage'. But perhaps this was not the time to poke the bull.

All the same, Jack couldn't help his reply.

"Does my father now have time for me, then?"

Giovani Lamnea Snr took a step towards his son and Jack instinctively squared his footing ready for a fight.

"Don't make me laugh, boy," said his father. "I'll have you on your back before you know it."

"A bigger man than you tried tonight," Jack threw back. "But he didn't manage it."

Immediately, he regretted saying it, but the old man had already seized upon it.

"I thought as much. Off fighting for money again. Well, it's better than those displays you give on the sands. Flexing your muscles and bending iron. I don't know why people crowd around you for it. They must be weak in the head."

Jack had been giving displays of his prowess on the Sands for the four months. It had started with him lifting his friends up, one hanging off each arm, and had developed into a sort of show – lifting heavy rocks, splitting them later with a hammer, arm wrestling and testing his strength against others from the Docks. His audience was equally split between men who envied him and women who wanted him and, although he had not started out with it in mind, Jack enjoyed the attention of both.

"I do it because I enjoy it," Jack replied. "And because they like to see it. Where's the harm in it? You know how hard it is working the docks, or the factory like Mam. So what if there's a little bit of fun at the end of the day? So what if the men want to try to better me and the women like to watch? It's no different to me playing rugby. What's it to you?"

Giovani spat on the floor between them. "It's unseemly. It brings our name down, lets people laugh at the antics of the Lamnea. You think it is just about you, but it's my name too. Your mother's name. Your brother. Your sister, Ellen – although now she is married she can hide the disgrace behind her husband's name."

Jack's fists were clenched by his side. It wasn't a new argument – he wished it was. He knew he could never win his father over. Despite having been in this country for over 30 years, Giovani's mind was still on the small island of Syros off the coast of Greece. Jack had never been there, but if he did, he imagined he would find it full of strait-laced people, hardworking but inflexible in their ways. Noble but stern. And everyone else would be a disappointment to them.

Jack stood much taller than the old man. Giovanni was 62 years old but still working as an Able Seaman on the *Prestonian*, a steamer that carried whatever was needed to wherever needed it. He had lied about his age to get the work, adding thirteen years to his birthdate, but he could get away with it. His muscular body was twisted by the hard work that had got him this far, by the graft that he had put in to survive in a foreign country. It could not have been easy starting a family in a strange land, and part of Jack admired that man – the family man, the honourable man. But all too often the face he presented these days was a bitter one. Of a man who was coming to the end of a hard life and who knew it. A man who clung to his name and reputation as the most important things left to him.

Unfortunately, Jack couldn't get him to see that his wrestling, his shows on Swansea Sands, his growing reputation, didn't harm the family name at all. If anything, it promoted it.

"So, hand over the money." His father's words snapped him back to the moment.

"What?" said Jack.

"If you are going to drag the family name through the mud, we should at least get the benefits from it. Give me your winnings."

Jack's mother stepped stood up. "Now Gio, there's no need for that. I'm sure Jack will use some of it for the rest of the family anyway."

"This is no concern of yours, Rovena," her husband snapped and she sat back down again.

Jack hated seeing his mother like this. She was a hard-working woman herself, spending long hours alongside his eldest sister at the Copperworks. They wouldn't have the house if she hadn't been working there – it was a company lodging, as they all were in the surrounding streets, and, although the Docks were technically there to service the incoming raw copper for smelting on site, he would not have been offered a house just on those grounds. It was worse for his father – as a seaman in the Mercantile Marine, he was away from home for long periods and the money he brought back was not enough to buy a house. He knew the old man was aware that the roof over his head wasn't something he himself had earned and he also knew that it ate him up inside.

"I'll give the money to Mum," Jack said, but his father shook his head.

"You'll give it to me."

He glanced at his mother. Out of sight of her husband, she gave a quick nod.

Jack pulled the money out of his trouser pocket. Five pounds. Hard earned and easily lost.

Giovanni took the money and stuffed it into his own pocket without a word.

"Now get to bed," he scowled.

When he had entered the house, the opportunity to lie in his own bed and relax his aching muscles was all that Jack had wanted. Now it seemed like giving in.

He winked at his mother and turned on his heel. As he stepped back out onto the street, he could hear the impotent fury of his father behind him.

*** 

It had been a bold move, but potentially a stupid one. Jack couldn't go back to the house that night. He knew that his father would sit up in the living room, watching the door until he fell asleep in his chair, waiting for the chance to lambast his son again or dreaming of winning the argument that would follow.

He could probably stay with Ellen. His sister lived only a few streets over. Her husband was a good man and he knew enough of Ellen's own problems at home to give Jack a space on the floor for the night. Turning up his collar against a night that suddenly seemed a lot less hospitable than it had earlier, Jack set off towards her house.

The streets were quieter now. No singing could be heard on the night breeze, no laughter. Everyone was home and in bed or passed out in a gutter somewhere. It felt like Jack had the whole world to himself.

He walked for a little while, happy in his own thoughts. The fight had been a good one. Most of the lads around the Docks had already tried their hand at beating him, either in feats of strength or in a wrestling bout, and he'd found there was something quite commonplace about them. They were enthusiastic amateurs with no skill, no grace. Tanner, however, was a veteran like himself. He could feel the memory of hundreds of throws in his stance. His opponent's every move had been created from the knowledge of moves that brought victory and mistakes that did not. It had been a fight that tested his experience against someone else's equal experience, and that had made it a memorable evening.

As he turned into his sister's street, Jack saw a figure up ahead of him. Something about the way the man was standing, looking up at the houses, made him look lost.

It was a surprise to see anyone on the streets at this time and more so for it to be a face that Jack did not know. The surprises continued, however, as he drew closer to the man.

"Jack? Jack Lamnea?"

Jack looked the man up and down. It was dark but he was evidently wearing fancier clothes than you would find on a dock worker outside of his wedding day.

"Yes," Jack replied. "You have me at a disadvantage…"

"We've never met," said the man, offering a hand to shake. "But I watched you fight tonight. Excellent work."

The man was Welsh but his accent wasn't local. "William Coutts," he said as they shook hands. "But call me Billy. I'm the manager of both the Palace Theatre and the Star Theatre in town."

Jack knew of the Palace Theatre, of course – Frank Owens seemed to spend all his time there when not organising fights or working – but he'd never been. The Star was an unknown quantity to him as it only put on plays and they'd always seemed a bit daunting to him. There was a slight echo of his father as he realised he thought it was a waste of money, a frippery he could do without.

Before Jack could say anything, Billy Coutts was jumping in again. "Now this may seem a little strange, but I'm actually walking the streets tonight looking for you. Well, I was – I think some of your friends sent me the wrong way as a joke. Very funny.

"You see, I want to make you an offer."

Jack looked suspiciously at him.

"Well, full disclosure – tonight wasn't the first time I've seen you. I first noticed you – or rather the crowds you were attracting – on the

Sands. I mean, what you do there, the weightlifting, it's incredible. I saw when you picked those four girls up, two hanging from each arm."

"You should have been there the next time," Jack said. "I did six."

"Brilliant!" Billy exclaimed. His enthusiasm was apparent even if the reason for his being there still wasn't.

"Well, I'd like to offer you the chance to do that again and get paid for it. Strongman acts are all the rage at the moment, and with you we've got our very own homegrown one! How'd you like three nights a week – one of them Saturday – on stage at the Palace as part of my Music Hall line up? You'd get a cut of the door take and you'd only be working 30 minutes a night at most."

"But what would I do?" Jack asked.

"Just what you're doing now! Feats of strength, trials of power. We can challenge members of the audience to better you, lift heavy weights. Perhaps even fight you. No? Well, we can discuss that bit. But just think of it – your name on a marquee. On a poster! Jack Lamnea – Strongman!" Billy was quite carried away with his sales pitch.

Jack stood in the street and thought about it. It was getting late in the year, so he knew he'd have to stop doing the Sands soon as the nights drew in. And this was guaranteed pay for doing something he loved anyway. There was only one problem. The same one he'd just walked out on.

"If I do it," he said cautiously, "I don't want to be Jack Lamnea. I'd rather be something else. Something local. How does Swansea Jack sound?"

Billy looked slightly disappointed but he knew a deal breaker when he heard one, so he nodded slowly. "Swansea Jack – Strongman. Yes, I think we can work with that."

Jack stuck out his hand again. But before he shook on the deal, another thought struck him. Something Frank Owens had said earlier on.

"How about Swansea Jack – the Welsh Hercules?"

Billy grinned in the darkness.

**Gladys Eliza Darke**

## Chapter Two

**1911**

The light was in his eyes.

His heart was pounding and the light was in his eyes and he felt stupid in this weird uncomfortable... costume. It was the only word for it. He tugged at the tight collar and felt a bead of sweat run down under the material and onto his chest.

The light was in his eyes and his heart was pounding and he could hear everybody out there. Whispering. Chatting. He didn't want to look, didn't want to turn around. Friends, relatives, they were all there, all watching. Well, all except one.

The light was in his eyes and his heart was pounding and then – frighteningly, mercifully – the music started. All the chatter stopped. For a moment, he thought that his timpani heart had stopped too. The light was still in his eyes, but a moment of calm fell upon him because the music could mean only one thing.

She was here.

Of course, he knew she would be, had to be, but still at the back of his head, he had been worried. Nothing had scared him as much as the thought that she might not walk through those doors. Not fighting, not performing on stage. Nothing was as worrying as life without her.

Jack Lamnea turned away from the light and greeted his bride as she walked through the Registry Office towards him.

*** 

They had met on stage.

The Welsh Hercules had become quite the hit in the local Music Halls. Billy Coutts had been as good as his word, got him work at the Palace Theatre of Varieties and even at the Star Theatre (although Jack was the first to say he was no actor. So far he had appeared as the henchman in two Pantos and played a non-speaking Rude Mechanical in a production of 'A Midsummer Night's Dream' - despite still not being sure what a Rude Mechanical was).

He had worked his way up the bill (and into the show – he now appeared 5 times a week) so that now his name was third on the red-lettered poster outside the Palace Theatre of Varieties - *Swansea's Own! The Welsh Hercules Performing Feats of Strength and Daring!*

Only Clarke & Glenny (*In The Laughable 'Haunted House'*) and Arthur St George (*Patriotic Vocalist*) were above him. He knew both turns well and there was no animosity about the billing – although one of them at least was a little annoyed about where Jack appeared in the show.

The Welsh Hercules had cornered the slot straight after the Electric Bioscope projection. The grainy black and white images, projected onto a screen suspended over the front of the stage, only lasted around 20 minutes, but they were one of the most popular parts of the evening. People crowded in to see news from around the country, sometimes from around the world, and Billy Coutts realised that, if he wanted them to stay, he had to open with a spectacular act straight after the films. Arthur St George argued that a patriotic singalong was the perfect companion act but Billy knew his audience. They wanted spectacle. They wanted something that would rival moving pictures of London and Manchester but which came from their own back yard. They wanted Jack.

And, of course, the strongman act could also set up behind the screen whilst the film was showing, meaning that there was no interruption to the programme and, as soon as the screen lifted, Jack could be revealed in all his glory, a veritable tableau vivant of strength.

It worked. The audience loved his depiction of Hercules Unchained (as the title card at the side of the stage proclaimed). As the screen rose, Jack was revealed to be bound by iron chains across his arms and chest, twisting and straining against them as two stagehands in 'authentic' Roman costumes (borrowed from a production of 'Julius Caesar' at the Star) pretended to whip him. By expanding his chest and flexing his biceps, Jack was able to break the chains and they would fall to the floor with a mighty thud, followed immediately by cheers from the audience.

It was a well-practised act but initially there had been one problem. To break the chains, Jack needed to not only flex but breathe in at the same time, filling his lungs and swelling his chest. But as the screen rose on his first night following the Bioscope, the air from the auditorium rushed in to greet him and brought with it the audience's accumulated stench of cigarette smoke, whisky fumes, sweat and farts.

All Jack could do was cough. Deep wracking coughs.

The audience found it hilarious. Various wags hurled insults at him – "Come on, they're only fake!", "I've thrown stronger fish back in the canal!" – and Jack knew it was only a matter of time before fruit and probably stones would follow. There was no way to go but forward. He took another deep breath, fought back the choking sensation it brought and flexed his chest with all the power he had.

The chains shattered. One link went flying into the audience and hit a man in the eye, causing a combination of awe and hilarity from the onlookers.

"Who thinks they're bloody fake now?" Jack yelled out to the audience, drawing himself up to his full height. Then, suddenly, all the air that he'd taken in wanted out and he followed his words with an even louder belch. The crowd loved it.

Hercules Unchained became a regular part of Jack's act after that.

At first, he'd been nervous on stage but, as time had gone by, Jack realised that he was starting to understand an audience. Billy had paired him with a comedian for his first few months – a scrawny man who wore the same leopard skin shorts and gold sash over his leggings as Jack did and who introduced the two of them to the audience as 'brothers'. The patter was all down to the comedian. Jack stayed mute and impassive as he lifted weights or threw the frightened man from one arm to the other. But as the weeks progressed, he started to learn where to put a glance or a double take to create a laugh of his own. After a little while, he asked the comedian if they could work out a little comedic routine between them, complete with dialogue, and so he became used to speaking on stage and projecting his voice.

Billy Coutts kept a close eye on this, of course. One night he came to Jack and told him that the comedian was ill and couldn't go on for that performance. Told him this about five minutes before his act was due to start. Jack remembered looking out from the wings at the magician on stage before him, all suave patter and sleight of hand, and thinking that he couldn't do it. For the first time in his life, thinking something was beyond him.

Yet he went on. He remembered Billy Coutt's hand on his back, and the lights on the stage, and then suddenly he was back in the wings with the sound of the audience cheering him. He had done it, complete with some patter of his own. And there to greet him as he left the stage was Billy, with his arm around the supposedly-ill comedian and a big grin on his face.

After that, Jack's confidence on stage grew. He was still a little wary of some parts of showbusiness – the guys were a little too forward sometimes and the women sometimes came across as the kind of girls his Mam warned him off – but on the whole, he loved it. The surge of adrenalin as he went on stage, the appreciative sound of the audience, the camaraderie of all the turns – a family away from home. It felt like somewhere he was meant to be. And it didn't hurt that he could make the same amount of money for three night's work at the Palace as he could in two weeks hard labour at the Docks.

But above all else, he loved the theatre because it had given him Gladys Eliza Darke.

The night he met her had been like any other. He had started with Hercules Unchained, then invited a male member of the audience up on stage. He had played with the idea that he'd brought him up to try wrestling him (the fear in the man's eyes had been real) but in the end just explained that he only wanted one thing from him: a penny. Then, having taken that and a shilling from the man, he tore each coin in half with his bare hands, sending the man back to his seat awestruck but poorer.

A few weightlifting demonstrations followed (after asking members of the audience to verify that the weights were indeed real) and then came the crowning glory of his act – the Wheel.

For this, a large cartwheel was brought out, solid and bound by steel, one side of it largely covered by a sheet of wood. As the two stagehands rolled it across the stage, the wheel almost as high as them, they fumbled it and the huge circular mass fell with a mighty bang that echoed around the auditorium. The audience were hushed immediately, and Jack assured them that they were perfectly safe, even though this was an extremely dangerous demonstration for him. He did not tell them that the stagehands dropped the wheel every night to create just this effect.

The wheel having been brought out, Jack would then announce that – at great personal risk to himself – he would lie on the stage and have the whole weight of the wheel placed on his chest. This usually provoked a few hushed ooh's. But then, he continued, he would – by sheer strength and willpower alone – support the further weight of not one, not two, but three women standing on top of the wheel. The audience were always suitably impressed by this claim.

Normally, Jack would lie down on the stage at this point and prepare himself whilst the stagehands would select three ladies from the audience. Except on this night, he did something strange. On this night, he chose the first lady himself.

Jack had noticed her earlier in the evening. Three rows back, sitting demurely with a taller man whose features were similar enough to be a brother rather than a suitor. At least, he hoped that was the case. Raven dark hair done up in a bun, strong features, a face that could light up the world with a smile or bring it crashing down with a frown. He'd never seen her before, but he knew that he had to get to know her.

The stagehands looked on in confusion as Jack reached down from the stage and helped to guide the woman up the steps. He noticed that she looked a little confused but mostly she was amused. Almost every other woman to come up on stage had been anxious, nervous; she was calmly taking it all in as if being up on stage was something that happened every day.

After the demonstration, while he was taking his applause in front of the three women and the now upright wheel, Jack did something else he had never done before. He turned his back to the audience, faced the women, and bowed to them too. As he straightened up, he saw a look of approval in the dark-haired woman's eyes.

As he helped to guide her down the stairs once more, Jack leaned in and whispered, "Would you do me the honour of visiting me in my dressing room after the show?"

If she was surprised, she didn't show it, but still she leaned in a little more herself and said quietly, "I don't think that would be appropriate. But I will meet you in the coffeehouse across the road when I leave here. My brother will accompany me."

Jack nodded his agreement before he stepped back onto centre stage for his final bow. 'Brother', he thought to himself, and a broad grin spread over his face.

*** 

They were at the Neath Fair when Jack finally asked the big question. The Hafod Copperworks, where Gladys worked, had laid on a charabanc to transport workers to and from the vast fair site and Jack, Gladys, her brother George and his long-standing girlfriend, Clara, had elected to go as a group. In theory, the two couples were each supposed to be patrolling the other and keeping activities within respectable boundaries; in reality, the pairs split up as soon as they arrived at the Bird In The Hand Field with the promise to meet again before leaving.

It was the first time Gladys had been to the fair without her parents. Everything was extra bright and colourful as a result, but she was especially entranced by the massive attraction at the heart of the fairground. A sign atop a huge steam organ playing jaunty music proclaimed it as *Henry Studt's Zoological Roundabout*. Surrounding this were elaborately painted wooden animals - elephants, giraffes, camels, creatures she had never seen outside of schoolbooks but now frozen before her in varnished splendour - all galloping their way through a circular route, each with giggling girls on their backs.

To one side of this wonder was a helter skelter that Gladys had already been on, and behind that was the Scenic Railway, which was also attracting quite a crowd. All around her were wonders and excitement – flimsy-looking seats, suspended from a central pole, that spun around and lifted out giving the illusion of flight; Venetian gondolas carrying lovers around a bumpy circular track, sumptuously painted railings giving the occupants a little privacy in which to sneak a kiss. There were games of skill and chance, and vendors selling toffee apples, fudge and fairy floss. It was dizzying and fascinating all at once.

The noise too was incredible, much louder than the copper works even. Showmen shouted out to attract new customers, competing with the wheezing music of steam organs and the screams of delight coming from patrons. Drunken men staggered from attraction to attraction, sometimes singing along to the music from the steam organs, sometimes stopping to wonder where they were. Further over, the sound of sheep, horses and cows could be heard alongside the cries of the auctioneer selling them off, and behind everything was the steady rhythmic panting of several steam engines, the beating hearts of many of the attractions.

Gladys loved all of it. Jack, however, had a sourer countenance.

She looked up at him. "Are you still pouting because the Town Council has banned Boxing Shows this year?" she asked.

"It's not pouting," Jack replied. "I could have won us some good money by beating some of those ruffians."

"Or you could have been boxed around the ears and sent home with your tail between your legs," Gladys replied. Jack looked at her in a way that suggested she was very much mistaken, but even at this early stage in their relationship he knew better than to directly contradict her. They made an odd couple, his tall frame dwarfing hers, her sculpted features showing up the thickening of his ears and brows from many wrestling matches, but there was an obvious affection there.

"We can go and watch the football soon," she said, throwing him a lifeline that he might enjoy. "I'm sure many of the showmen you wanted to best will be in the South Wales team, so you can at least flex your muscles at them there."

Jack scowled a little but if he was honest that would have been the main reason for watching the match. He'd never really seen the attraction in football, not compared to his beloved rugby.

When the match came around, though, in the relative quiet of a nearby field, Jack realised that this was the perfect place to talk to Gladys. Something had been on his mind for a little while now and he couldn't put it off any longer.

"Gladys," he said, looking down at his sweetheart. "We've been walking out together now for five weeks."

Gladys looked at him. She knew there was more to come than just a display of timekeeping skills, but she also knew him well enough to wait.

"I think the time has come," he said, carefully, "for you to meet my family."

Gladys frowned. She already knew his mother from work, and he had introduced her to his sister when they had met in the street one day.

"Formally," Jack continued. "And completely."

The penny dropped. Jack wanted her to meet his father.

He didn't talk about Giovani Snr very much and when he did it was usually in a dark tone. Gladys knew that the father was not very happy with his son, but she had never delved into the reasons why, sensing that Jack would tell her in his own time. Now it seemed he had jumped over the explanation and gone straight to the demonstration.

"How would next Thursday be for you?" he asked, as if it was the most normal thing in the world, and all Gladys could do in return was nod.

A shout from the crowd brought Jack back to the football match and he joined in with the berating of the referee. Question asked, answer given. Evidently the subject was closed.

\*\*\*

Giovani Snr – John to his work colleagues, just as his son, named after him, had taken the easier route of Jack – was shorter than she expected.

Not that he was a small man – even sat in his chair, it was obvious he still had at least 6 inches over Gladys – but her perception of him until now had been filtered through Jack's reactions to his father and they presented a bleak, larger than life figure. This impression was reinforced by the gloom he now surrounded himself with, lit only by the flicker of the fire he was sat next to, shrouded in shadows. Over the fireplace, Gladys noticed two large, curved swords, glinting in the light. They looked out of place in the general austerity of the room and the way the light caught their blades was slightly threatening.

Gladys had been brought into the house and welcomed by Mrs Lamnea ("Call me Rovena, love") who had then introduced her other son, George. At 16, it was obvious that George would be more like his father in looks and stature than Jack ever was, but his temperament seemed to come from his mother. He shook Gladys' hand nervously and then retreated to a corner of the room obviously far away from Giovani Snr, nervously pushing an errant kiss curl away from his forehead.

Jack himself had barely said a word beyond introducing his mother and even then his eyes had barely left his father. Gladys was also aware that, consciously or not, he was now standing slightly in front of her and to her side, as if ready to step forward and protect her at any moment. The thought rather pleased her.

"Good evening, Mr Lamnea", she said, extending a hand in greeting.

Giovani Snr looked at her for a moment, realising that to shake her hand he would have to stand up from his chair and move towards the young woman. Gladys knew that this was the case too, but she resolutely did not move to meet him.

The hand remained outstretched. Giovani Snr glanced at his wife, who seemed to be studiously avoiding the scene, and then stood. He grasped Gladys' hand, gave it a quick up / down shake and then slumped back in his seat. He refused to look over at his son in case he saw him smiling.

Jack considered it more of a gentle smirk.

For the rest of her stay, Gladys and Giovani Snr stayed politely distant from one another, both in geography and conversation. As they all sat around the kitchen table and Jack's mother produced tea and freshly made scones for everyone, the conversation flowed, covering everything from Gladys' work at the Copperworks to her father's work on the railway to George's new job alongside his brother in the Docks. Gladys did try to introduce the topic of Neath Fair into the mix, but a grunt and a scowl from Jack's father put an end to that.

Hoping to lighten the mood a little, Gladys addressed the Lamnea patriarch directly. "I understand," she said, "that you came over here from Syros. In the Cyclades?"

Giovani Snr looked up and for the first time she thought she saw a flicker of interest in her in his eyes.

"I understand it is a beautiful island," she continued. A brief glance at Jack suggested that this was a good topic of conversation.

"It is the greatest of the islands," Giovani Snr growled. "So beautiful. So much sunshine. And the beaches, second to none. I wish I had not had to leave it for this rain-sodden land."

"Why did you leave?" Gladys asked, too late noticing the flash of warning that had come into the eyes of Jack's mother.

"Steam," said the old man. "Steam destroyed us. We were the most powerful port in the Aegean. Everybody brought their silks to us, their leather, everything the world needed when they travelled by sail. We were rich. My father, Efstate Lamnea, was a prominent merchant in

Ermoupoli. He had two houses. Two! On an island! These swords," he gestured upwards without looking, "were his, a gift from a Turkish merchant. He was loved and respected by all.

"But then the steamships came, and they didn't need Syros anymore. They sailed past us, on to Patras." He virtually spat the word out. "It killed the island. I watched as my father lost first one house and then the other. I saw him unable to look after his family. He had always worked, hard work, but the light went out in his eyes. When he died a poor man, I could not stay. I knew that if I had to support a family, I needed to go amongst the *allodapos*. And so I came here and I have worked hard every day."

Gladys glanced at Jack. His face said he had heard this story many times. Silently, he placed his hand over hers. Gladys had no idea what to say in response to Giovani Snr's words, so she stayed quiet. In retrospect, she decided that might have been a mistake.

"Hard work is the only way to go forward in this life," the old man continued. "Sweat and time. That is what you need to give to make it here. Sweat and time. There are no short cuts. No parading in front of strangers, so that they can laugh at you and call you names. That is not work. That is embarrassing."

Gladys felt Jack's hand tighten over hers and she could only imagine what was going through his head.

"Jack works hard too," she said. "He works at the Docks for a fair wage and then he works again at night in the theatre. No one laughs at him."

Giovani Snr looked her directly in the eyes, the first time he had done so since her arrival.

"I laugh at him," he said. "That a son of mine should come to this. And to be defended by a woman!"

A chair hit the floor as Jack stood up. He towered over the older man, but his father didn't seem to notice.

"Another act," he said, before slowly standing himself. Jack's fists were clenched by his sides and Gladys felt as if his silence and stillness at that moment were probably the strongest thing she had ever seen him do.

Giovani Snr turned away from everyone without even looking at his son and left the room through the back door. A few seconds later, they heard the door to the outhouse slam to.

"I'm sorry," Jack's mother began, but Jack just shook his head.

"We're going," he said and held out a hand to Gladys. She took it, noting how clammy with sweat it now was, and said her goodbyes to the remaining family. As they left the house, she wondered if the two men would ever – *could* ever – reconcile.

\*\*\*

The Palace Theatre was an unusual building, situated at the junction of two streets and looking like a wedge driven between them both. The actual theatre was on the first floor, with a Bar Parlour and Smoking Room taking up most of the street level (along with an unseen Manager's Office, Dressing Rooms for the turns and a kitchen). It was here that Billy Coutts suggested they hold the Wedding Reception. It was a kind gesture which saved Jack and his new bride the price of another venue, and a shrewd one because it meant Billy could keep an eye on all of his acts and ensure they were not too worse for wear to perform later that evening.

Billy was very proud of his work at the Palace and the nearby Star Theatre. They were not the only theatres in town, or the biggest (the new Empire held that distinction) but they were successful and, he liked to think, the most popular venues in town. This was partly because he was a master at publicity for the Variety Hall.

When Charlie Chaplin had recently joined Fred Karno's Army in America and looked set to have a career in films, Billy put an ad in the Swansea Gazette & Daily Shipping Register to remind everyone that he had played The Palace Theatre first (Billy neglected to mention that Chaplin had only been ten years old at the time – marketing, like Poker, was all about what to lead with and what to hold). Similarly, the names of Lillie Langtry and Marie Lloyd were prominent in the foyer of the Theatre, despite having only played there a handful of times years ago. Billy knew that he'd never have great stars on his stage when they were at the height of their prowess, but he was canny enough to realise that he could catch them on the way up (or occasionally, on the way down) and the talent would be the same. Even better, it cost less.

Billy looked over at the happy couple. Jack was toasting everyone, but the Manager had no worries that he would be unable to perform on stage that night. Jack had wholeheartedly embraced the Temperance Movement as part of his fitness regime – something that normally Billy would have disliked as it meant a lower bar take - and the strongest tipple he was likely to sample that night was Sarsaparilla. Briefly, Billy wondered if he should have offered the strongman the night off, as it was his wedding night, but he knew that was just sentimentality talking and sentimentality didn't run a theatre.

Scanning the crowd, Billy watched the rest of his troupe of performers cheer the new Mrs Lamnea. Arthur St George was evidently working himself up to sing a rousing anthem to the crowd, but Billy knew that the hit of the night would be Florrie Sanders, *The Saucy Soubrette*, who would regale everybody with a filthy ditty carefully crafted to include the happy couple.

Billy's gaze fell on the old Mrs Lamnea, Jack's mother, sat alone in a corner of the room. He went across to speak to her.

"Can I get you another drink, Mrs Lamnea?", he said.

Rovena Lamnea looked up at him and shook her head. She knew Billy Coutts (and knew even more about him thanks to what Jack had told her) and quite liked him.

"Haven't seen you in the audience for a while," Billy continued, undaunted. He pulled up a stool from the next table and sat down beside her. "Are we starting to bore you?"

"Oh, no, Mr Coutts -," she began.

"Billy," he cut in. "Call me Billy,"

"No... Billy", said Rovena, trying out the new familiarity. "I just don't get the chance to come as often as I'd like." There was a pause. "He doesn't like me going."

For a moment, Billy thought that she meant Jack. Then he realised.

"Mr. Lamnea?"

Rovena nodded.

"Is he here tonight?" Billy asked. "I'm always happy to make a convert, even if it costs me a Comp ticket."

"No," Rovena said, looking down at the floor. "He didn't come."

"To the Reception?" Billy said but before the words had left his mouth, the truth hit him. "He didn't go to his son's wedding, did he?"

Rovena neither confirmed nor denied his words but the answer was obvious.

Billy looked back across to Jack again. The big man was lifting his bride up over his head and laughing, just as she protested the action with giggles and playful slaps. If he was concerned about his father's absence, it didn't show. But then, Billy had not known of a rift between them anyway. Jack was always a very private man – rare among the turns, who knew everybody's business immediately and wasted no time broadcasting it – but even so, he had not had an inkling of trouble at home.

Immediately after this came another thought. He knew that the newlyweds didn't have the money to get a place of their own yet. Jack had recently left the docks to work as a smelter at the British Mannesmann Tube company in nearby Landore. It paid better than his old job, despite being backbreaking work, but it still wasn't enough. Feeding the furnaces was hard and tiring work and Billy had been concerned at first that Jack would have been too exhausted at the end of the day to perform on stage, but it didn't seem to bother him and if anything the work improved his muscular definition, which in turn was good for the act.

Jack had talked to Billy about a raise so that he could put down a deposit on somewhere of their own, but the promoter had been unable to help. So, he knew that they were, at least for the immediate future, staying with his parents, in the room that Jack had shared with his brother until this night. Suddenly, he was quite pleased that he hadn't given Jack the night off – the longer they had before they had to return to that atmosphere, the better. Billy wondered too if Jack's new job was just a financial move or if it had been prompted by a desire to get away from Lamnea Snr at work as well.

"I'm sorry," said Billy. "I didn't realise."

"We married in a church," Jack's mother continued. "It was over in Cardiff. There was no Greek Orthodox Church at the time - five years ago, they built the current one. So, we had to get married in the Norwegian Church back then. It was a proper ceremony though, a lovely day. Giovani was so handsome, so proud. It was important to him to be married in an Orthodox ceremony."

Rovena smiled at him. "He's not a bad man," she said. "He just sees things a different way. Different values. I suppose it happens with every generation. He's proud, just like his son. And that's the problem."

"Well, from my point of view," Billy replied, "he – both of you – should be proud of your son. He'll be a good husband to that young woman and no doubt a good father. It's a shame Mr Lamnea doesn't want to be part of that."

Rovena Lamnea took his hand for a moment, holding it gently.

"Oh, he wants to," she said. "I just don't think he knows how anymore."

And with that, she let go of his hand and stood up. "I'll be expected at home," she said. "I'll get the room ready for Jack. It was lovely to speak to you, Mr... Billy."

After she had gone, Billy stayed sat in the corner of the bar for a little longer. Then, after Florrie's song was over and the magician had produced a special bouquet for Gladys, after Jack had kissed his bride and told her in front of everyone how much he loved her, after he had thought how little anyone truly knew about another, Billy stood up and glanced at his pocket watch.

Enough thinking. It was showtime!

Battle Cruiser Rugby Competition

HMS LION

J.L.LAMNEA

# Chapter Three

## May 1916

A cold wind was blowing in off the Firth of Forth but Jack and the rest of the crew working alongside him didn't notice it. There was far too much to be done.

3,600 tons of coal had to be loaded aboard ship, moved from the Rosyth dockyard where they were berthed to the very bowels of *HMS Lion*. It was hard, back-breaking work and something the whole ship was begrudgingly involved in. For once, Stoker Second Class Jack Lamnea wasn't just one of the dust monkeys working below, he was part of the crew - everyone levelled by the filth and pressure of having to get the ship sea-worthy.

Not that this would be a long-lasting truce. The Navy was scrupulous about the ship being clean and jobs such as this – coaling - meant that even when the ship was fully stocked the work would continue. Hessian sheets had been laid down across every surface on deck in an effort to stop the coal dust from spreading, but it was a thankless task. Guns were carpeted and doors had been locked firmly shut to protect the compartments and mess decks below, yet the dust was ever present.

Hatches that were normally sealed to keep water from getting in would be opened later to reveal inches of black dust piled up beyond them. No one enjoyed the clean up after coaling, and to a man the crew put the blame for the extra work on the Stokers.

The dockside crane swung another net full of coal sacks towards the loading hatch and Jack could see a faint trail of soot following its arc. The wind took some of it, but still the coal dust fell like black snow on everyone.

Jack looked around him. Faces were familiar but rank was almost impossible to tell. Stokers wore a uniform for coaling but everyone else wore either old overalls or old civilian clothes so that their naval uniform stayed clean. The only people he knew would be in full uniform were up on the Bridge, windows closed away from the mess. Vice Admiral David Beatty, now physically distant from his men (although his public school attitude and self-designed uniform had always kept him apart), would be chief amongst them.

Jack had been working for three hours already and at this point it was getting difficult to tell where his sleeves ended and skin began. Everyone was filthy, coal dust in their hair and smeared across their skin, thick black caked into their clothes. It looks like a carnival for chimney sweeps, Jack thought with a wry smile. Junior officers, cadets, midshipmen and sailors all toiling away at the same job, distinctions temporarily forgotten.

Jack looked up as the net full of coal sacks swung his way. He was standing at the entrance to the upper coal bunker, and it was his job to help centre the load and open the coal for delivery below. In some ways, this was one of the few times that his height had proved an advantage on board. Some stokers worked as Trimmers inside the bunkers like this one and the lower bunker below it. It was their job to spread the delivered coal evenly, so as not to upset the trim of the ship, but there was not a lot of space in the bunkers and Jack's huge stature made him a liability rather than an asset in those conditions. Even then, it was dangerous work. Jack had been detailed to help once when he first started on board *HMS Lion*, but the dust was so thick down there and the light so scarce it was like swimming through mud. Teams of men shovelled the deposited coal as more came thundering down the chute towards them – if they weren't quick enough, it would overtake them, and Jack knew of men who had been buried underneath a delivery. Not all of them survived.

Not that his own role was without its dangers. Delivering the coal from the end of a crane was not an exact science and the weight of the loaded net could sweep a man into the bunker or even overboard, where the icy Scottish waters of the Forth would easily finish him off if rescue wasn't quick. Even a glancing blow at the wrong angle could break bones. But Jack actually felt happy doing this job. It reminded him of when he worked on the docks at Swansea and talking with the crane drivers there. It was a little connection to memories of home.

"Behind you, Herc!" yelled a voice and Jack instinctively ducked. The cargo of coal swung gracefully past him but as it did Jack noticed what the call had been for. A large piece of hessian was sticking out from the netting, having come loose during the loading. In itself, it probably wouldn't have unbalanced him, but it was wet and rough and the coal dust encrusted in it gave it a sharp edge – if it had caught him in the face, he'd have had a nasty cut.

Jack looked across at the caller, Artificer First Class Roland Sweet. His normally blonde hair was uncharacteristically dark now but the cheeky smile was a clear indicator of who he was. Jack had worked with the man down below and they got on well together. He nodded his thanks to him and waited for the net to swing back in his direction.

Feet firmly planted, he grabbed at the netting and caught it. No one else there would have been able to slow the movement of such a pendulum, but Jack – Herc to his mates, after he'd told them about his Music Hall days – was one of the strongest men on board. Even so, the momentum wrenched at his arms and he knew that he couldn't stop it completely. Jack let go, but the wide pendulum swing had been halted and the next time the coal came close, he was able to stop it and drag it into place over by the bunker hole.

Quickly, Jack undid the hook from the net and signalled for the crane driver to take the hawser away. As he did, the coal settled at his feet, ten two-hundredweight bags. If they had been coaling at sea or the cranes had not been available, each man on board would have been expected to carry one hundredweight bag onto the deck for depositing in the bunker. The crane allowed for larger bags but also meant that Jack had a heavier load to lift.

"Look out below!" the foreman yelled into the darkness at their feet. A faint 'Aye!' was heard in return and Jack grabbed the first bag, half dragging, half throwing it to the edge of the bunker hole. He quickly undid the rope tying the top and poured the contents into the gloom. Once empty, he returned for the next bag.

Three hours in. At least 7 more hours to go, and then only if there were no major accidents. Yet no one complained.

This wasn't like a normal coaling. Everyone knew the voyage they were preparing for had a purpose.

In two days, they and the rest of the fleet would leave Scotland and set sail for the coast of Denmark.

And there they would win the war.

\*\*\*

Jack had never intended to go to war. He had joined the Royal Naval Volunteer Reserve simply because they had a gym.

It had been 1913 and, although there were rumblings of a conflict in Europe on the horizon, none of it really seemed to apply to Swansea. The idea of battle seemed even further away on the stage of the newly-renamed Swansea Popular Picture Hall and People's Palace. Billy Coutts had finally bowed to the popularity of cinema in the town and changed the billing – and priorities - for his own venue. It meant that there were fewer live acts on the stage now, but The Welsh Hercules was still a favourite, even if he did go back to just three nights a week.

For Jack, the biggest problem with this change was not a loss in earnings – he still had his work at the foundry, after all – but the fact that for four nights a week, he was now expected to be at home. Home, where he lived with Gladys (heavily pregnant at the time with his second child, Winifred), his one-year-old daughter Lily, his mother and, of course, the scowling figure of his father. Between the judgemental silence of the old man and the shrill crying of the baby, Jack desperately needed something else to do and somewhere else to be. An adherence to Temperance (despite the new temptations otherwise) meant that he had little interest in spending all his evenings in the pub with the other dockers, but still he needed an escape.

His days of illegal wrestling were behind him now – partly because Gladys frowned on it and partly because Billy Coutts had warned him against it for fear that an injury might forfeit his place in the show. So, when Wynn Evans, a fellow docker, told Jack about the RNVR it caught his attention. At first, he had some doubts – you had to sign up to the service for three years and, apart from learning the rules of the Navy, it seemed to mainly be training in shooting and sailing, with two weeks a year spent at a Naval base for further instruction – but when Wynn mentioned how the Commander was an avid follower of the teachings of Sandow and had installed a gymnasium for all recruits, the deal was struck. Jack knew of the great strongman Eugen Sandow and had even taken on some of his famous *System of Physical Training*, but he had never come across anyone else who had wanted to push themselves to achieve Sandow's Grecian Ideal. Suddenly, the Voluntary Reserve looked like the perfect way to increase his strength, improve his act and get some much-needed time away from home.

Three days later, Jack had signed up. He had access to a new set of weights and, in the Commander, a gym partner who was willing to push him and get extra equipment as needed. He even shared Jack's regime of fasting one day a week to help purify the body. Life was good.

Joining the RNVR had one other unexpected side effect as well – his father actually approved of something he had done. Jack didn't emphasise the weight training when he was around Giovani Snr, but from what he could tell the old man had no problems with it anyway. Having only recently – and begrudgingly - left the Mercantile Marine through ill health, Giovani had always extolled the virtues of comradeship and hard work that came with a life at sea. Now that Jack was part of the Naval forces, even in a distanced way, he realised that, for probably the first time in his life, his father felt like they shared a common experience.

Matters became much more serious, however, when war was declared in July of the following year. At first, no one knew what would happen. Rumours were rife, but Jack just continued his training and exercising as normal in Swansea. Gladys worried about him being called up to fight but Jack assured her that the professional Reserves, the old seamen and retired members of the Merchant Navy, would be called first. By Christmas, he told her, it would all be over.

But it wasn't. And they were almost at the second Christmas of the War before Jack got the call to present himself at *HMS Vivid* in Devonport.

He had been to *Vivid* before and this call, like all his others, was presented as just another two week training session. As a Stoker - a position his Commander had chosen for him because of his strength and his experience feeding the furnaces at Landore - Jack had to present at *Vivid II* alongside other Stokers and Artificers. Despite the name, *HMS Vivid* was not a ship. It was a set of barracks and training grounds, split between the engineering recruits in *Vivid II* and the Seamen, Signalling and Telegraphy recruits in *Vivid I*. Jack hated it.

It was not so much the sudden immersion into Naval Rules that he disliked, it was the fact that this seemed to go hand in hand with chaos and violence as soon as the training day ended. Hundreds of men from all across the British Isles were barracked together in conditions that seemed to have been based on a prison ship. Berths were packed into large open rooms with no ventilation or heating and everyone was given meagre rations, leading to jostling for food and outright theft from those hungry enough to risk it. Combined with the exhaustion that many felt from the tough training schedule, and the fact that regional differences between the men often led to disagreements, the barracks became a powder keg just waiting for the spark.

On his very first night at *Vivid*, two years earlier, Jack witnessed three fights, one of which had ended in a man having to fix his own broken nose. Nobody wanted to fight Jack, for obvious reasons, but he noted that the younger or newer recruits were frequently the ones being picked on. One young man spent most of that night cowering in a corner of the barracks and crying, saying over and over that he just wanted to go home.

Over the course of that initial two-week visit, Jack became a protector by default to some of the new recruits who were being bullied. He couldn't look after all of them, but he was able to provide a deterrent to some of the older hands. He only got into one fight, with a particularly belligerent Geordie, but it was short-lived and taught everyone not to mess with him or his charges again. Even so, men returning drunk from shore leave or angry about gambling losses caused upset on every night of his stay.

On his second visit to *Vivid*, Jack found that, despite being with a different set of men, nothing had changed. Once again, he was forced to play protector and once again he was able to put down the biggest bully – only this time, he sought him out and knocked him flat before things got out of hand. As it turned out, however, this heroic act was not needed – four days into his stay, one of the recruits returned from shore with what was later identified as influenza. Within a day, a third of the barracks had come down with it. By the next day, it was more than half. There was no more fighting and Jack, along with many men, took to sleeping outside if they could. Luckily, he never contracted the illness.

So, on his latest posting to *Vivid*, Jack was expecting more of the same, at least in terms of the violence.

Instead, on his arrival, he was somewhat shocked to be presented with his mobilization papers, proclaiming him fit and ready for active duty. Alongside this, he was given a pre-written postcard to send back home, informing them that he was leaving 'tomorrow, destination unknown'. Welcome to the war.

This new situation brought with it an increased wage of 2 shillings per day – Stokers were one of the best paid ranks in the Navy – but this was immediately undercut by a weekly charge for Jack's uniform, bedding and food rations. If he wanted to supplement the basic rations the Navy supplied or even get a haircut, Jack knew he would need most of the money that was left, which in turn meant there would be very little left to send home to Gladys.

The other thing Jack received was his Stoker's Manual. This was a hundred-page book setting out the basics of Boilers, Furnaces, Engines and Turbines with detailed diagrams and passages on how to watch the Temperature, Steam, Water and Oil gauges. As a Stoker Second Class, Jack didn't need to know all the details of how to run an engine, but he did have to have a strong working knowledge of it. A mistake at any level of a Stoker's job could result in injury or even death. In the best-case scenario, this only applied to the Stoker himself; in the worst, it could sink the ship.

Jack, however, was not a great reader. He knew his alphabet and could read some passages from the Bible; he had even, with great care, read his contract for the Music Hall, but none of it came easily to him. The diagrams helped him in his studies – some of the boiler parts found in it had even been manufactured by his old employer - but it was still hard going. However, he was pleased to see that when he needed it most, some of his earlier kindness came back to help him. A young Stoker named Williams, who was himself studying to be a Leading Stoker, recognised Jack as the man who had helped him escape a beating two years before. He noticed how slowly Jack appeared to be reading the Manual and cautiously offered to assist him with the training. In truth, the poor lad was half expecting a beating for suggesting a weakness in the big man, but Jack saw it for the kind act it was and very gratefully accepted.

In stark contrast to the past, these two weeks at *Vivid* flew by. Alongside his training for looking after the engines of a ship, Jack also had to take lessons in parade drill, rifle drill, housekeeping and naval history. It was exhausting and thankfully kept his mind away from worrying about his family back in Wales. He knew that Gladys would be distraught when she got the news that he was not returning and he wished that he'd known before leaving home, so that he could have said goodbye properly. He didn't like to think of what would happen if he didn't come back from the war, but he knew that a naval pension would not be enough on its own to support a young family. Ironically enough, his only hope in all this was that his father would look after them, proud in the knowledge that his son was going off to fight for his adopted country.

At the end of the two weeks, Jack got to find out which ship he would be assigned to. The answer amazed him.

*HMS Lion* was the flagship of England's Battle Cruiser fleet. The fastest ship of the day, able to reach a speed of up to 28 knots, she was also the command ship for Vice Admiral David Beatty and carried with her all the prestige that this brought. Stronger, faster and better armed than the *Indefatigable* class of battle cruisers that came before her, *HMS Lion* had proved her status by sinking the German light cruiser *Cöln* at the Battle of Heligoland Bight the previous year. She was a very impressive ship – but more importantly to sailors, she was also a lucky one.

This reputation, officially frowned upon but quietly encouraged to raise morale, was as a result of her actions at the Battle Of Dogger Bank earlier that year. During this battle, *Lion* was hit 16 times by enemy shells. It was not unknown for one direct hit to sink a ship, so this in itself was seen as a miracle. Several of *Lion*'s coal bunkers had been flooded, two out of her three dynamos had been shorted and the auxiliary condenser had also been flooded. Her hull was punctured numerous times and at one point, in the heat of battle, she lost all power. When the encounter was over, she had to be towed back to port by her sister ship, *HMS Indomitable*, and had since spent several months at Rosyth being refitted. By all accounts, she should have been at the bottom of the North Sea. Yet despite this, out of a crew of over 1000 sailors, only one man died during the battle and only 20 wounded were reported. She was, indeed, a lucky ship.

Jack wasn't a great one for superstition, but even he could see that the odds had definitely favoured his new ship (although he hoped that this good fortune actually came about through equally good design and leadership).

Jack was taken to Rosyth to join *Lion* and spent 6 months with her before the order came through to prepare for an important campaign of action. It proved to be an interesting time.

For a start, despite having grown up around docks and been with the Voluntary Reserves for over two years, Jack had never actually been on a ship before. The odd boat in Swansea harbour, yes

– but a 700 ft long steel juggernaut ploughing through seas where the waves were higher than the steeple of Pantygwydr Baptist Church, that was something else! Despite this, it didn't take him long to get his sea legs. After vomiting up everything he had eaten for apparently the last two months, he was thrown into his work on board. There was no time to allow him to be ill, so Jack had to just press on through it and somewhere in between frequent trips to the head and lying as still as he could on his bunk, he realised that he was starting to anticipate the movements of the ship and learn how to roll with the swell of the sea. There was still the occasional queasy moment, but on the whole he got used to the weird movement of his new home (and was secretly pleased that even the oldest of hands on board sometimes suffered that way too).

Life on *Lion* took some getting used to as well. A lot of Jack's time was spent in the Engine and Boiler Rooms in the depths of the ship. The work was hard physical labour for the most part and his days were a sequence of hardships and discomfort, veering wildly been severe danger and crushing monotony. Jack's job for the first six months on board was that of Coal Trimmer. In partnership with another Stoker, it was his job to fill a steel box called a skid with coal and then transport this from the coal bunker to the furnace. The skid, which resembled some form of mutant pram crossed with a sled, held about two hundredweight of coal, and weighed much the same again when empty. The journey from the bunker to the furnace took around ten minutes in good conditions, with one stoker pulling the skid with a rope while the other pushed it from behind. The skid was on sled runners rather than wheels to give it more stability as the ship fought its way through rough seas – or at least that was the theory. Jack and his fellow Stoker still had to fight to keep it upright at times, and if they failed, they had to right the Skid and refill it again to start over.

The coal was emptied onto the deck in front of the furnace and from there another Stoker would shovel the material into the blazing maw. It was this position, firing the boilers, that Jack would move into after his apprenticeship as a Coal Trimmer and, even though this was backbreaking work in itself, he couldn't wait. As it was, by the time they had got the skid back to the bunker and refilled it, and then got the new load back to the furnace, their original delivery would be completely used up, meaning that they were in a state of constant motion if the ship was to keep moving.

Jack worked a four-hour shift as a Coal Trimmer, with eight hours off to sleep. Not that he got eight hours sleep. The dust in the bunkers was so thick it clogged up his lungs and at the end of his shift he would spend at least a quarter of an hour just hawking up black sediment from in his throat. It would be another half hour before he had the strength to bathe himself in the Stokers' bathroom, in a forlorn effort to get the black dust off him. No matter how hard he scrubbed, there was always a grey pallor to his skin. But even then, he was not allowed to rest. As soon as he had showered, Jack, like every worker in the stokehole, was required to dress in a dry, clean uniform and be inspected by the Chief Stoker of the watch before they were free to go down to the mess-deck to eat and sleep. Navy rules.

It was thankless work, yet like all the Stokers, Jack took pride in it. Before the end of every shift, he would ensure that everything was set up for the next team even if he was exhausted. White hot clinker would need to be removed from the furnaces, hosed down with sea water to allow it to be moved and then transported in a skid to the Ash Ejector, which was about five minutes hard slog away. Sometimes this job could be combined with the delivery of the coal, meaning a fully laden skid had to be manoeuvred both ways through the ship.

Yet the Stokers of *HMS Lion* also had one other feature, beyond their determination, that helped them get through their shifts – they sang. Jack at first wondered if this was because quite a few Stokers had been miners prior to joining up, and fellow Welshmen at that, but apparently the habit of singing as they worked was peculiar to the *Lion* and had been going on for longer than he had been there. Even in the furnace room, where the heat took the saliva from inside your mouth and the noise drowned out all else, they sang. Hymns, bawdy ditties, crowd pleasers that he recognised from the Music Hall – it didn't matter what the song was, everyone joined in.

Jack enjoyed the singing. He knew he didn't have a good voice, but neither did most of the men in the stokehole. It gave them something in common, a camaraderie that was worth more than the words they shared and which separated them from the other ranks and departments of the ship. In the dull monotony of moving the skid from one place to another, it provided a little light relief.

And, probably most importantly, it definitely wasn't in the Navy Rules.

This was the life Jack knew for most of his stay in the Navy. For his first six months, *Lion* was on patrol in the North Sea or berthed in her dock at Rosyth, a figurehead for the Service and a visible reminder of Britain's seagoing supremacy. Until the call came, Jack hadn't seen any action with her. He was in the curious position of both wanting to go to battle and fearing the outcome – every day was filled with morale boosting and jingoistic news from the Navy, but around him he could see the survivors of Dogger Bank and other campaigns and he knew the true cost of war.

In the end, however, as he and everyone on board knew, the decision would not be his.

At least when the information came through, it was explained that they would be taking part in a defining moment for Britain and the war, a new Trafalgar. 151 Allied ships would set sail, carrying over 100,000 men, led by Admiral Sir John Jellicoe and their own Vice Admiral Beatty. They would engage with the Germans and win.

It was to be a glorious enterprise.

Once it was over, the Danish peninsula of Jutland would be remembered forever in the history of warfare.

Portrait of Jack and Gladys in 1916

## Chapter Four

### 1st June 1916

Jack had no idea what was happening. Nobody below decks did.

Before they went into battle, Jack had spoken to some of the veteran crew members about what to expect. Their answers ranged from the hopeful to the fatalistic, but no amount of talking could have prepared him anyway. He clung to the best piece of advice he'd heard – *Do the job you are supposed to do, trust in others doing theirs.*

Even concentrating on the task in hand, though, was difficult.

Every time one of the ship's twin guns fired, the whole vessel would be briefly lifted higher in the water by the recoil, before settling again moments later. The sea, relatively calm earlier, was now choppy from the action taking place upon it, meaning that no footstep could be taken safely. To make it worse, every time the ship lifted and settled, new clouds of coal dust rose up, making it difficult to see and even more difficult to breathe. Originally, Jack had worn a strip of cloth around his mouth and nose to help keep the dust out but, when he reached the furnaces with his skid of coal, the heat was so great that the cloth made breathing even more difficult and eventually he abandoned it altogether.

All this was hard enough but the constant noise was even worse. Some Stokers had told him to plug his ears with bits of cloth or even wax, but he had not heeded their words. That had been a mistake. Jack thought that the roar of the furnaces working to bring the ship to full speed was possibly the loudest thing he had ever heard. It was a constant roll of thunder, seeming to fill every space he entered, until the booming lightning of another gun going off would drown even this out. There was no singing now, no conversation. Commands usually sent down through the speaking tube were useless – ship's telegraph was now the only way to communicate with anyone. Even then, the bell that signalled a new command or change in direction could not be heard, so the Leading Stoker needed to be watching it at all times.

*Do the job you are supposed to. Trust in others doing theirs.*

Jack repeated the phrase in his head. He needed something to concentrate his mind on the task in hand. In the very back of his mind, he was aware that, if the ship was struck by a shell or a torpedo, he and everyone around him would be dead. Forget that they were below the water line and that this was the exact area torpedoes were sent to hit; ignore the fact that all the doors to the upper decks were firmly closed and sealed, meaning that no one here would have time to escape; the real threat came because the furnaces were close to the magazines for the great guns, and they were the prime target of the enemy. A direct hit there could break the ship in two.

All the Stokers knew the truth. Even with bullets and shells whizzing down around you and fires raging by your side, the safest place to be in battle was on deck. At least there you had a chance of getting off a sinking ship.

Time had no meaning. Jack had started his shift before the first salvo had been fired. The exhausted men he had taken over from had seemed surprised to see him. He now knew why. That could have been an hour ago or he could be about to be relieved himself – he placed his faith in the strict regularity of naval life and hoped that his own replacements weren't injured (or worse) somewhere else.

As another explosion from the guns resounded through the ship, Jack's skid lurched violently to one side. He was at the front, pulling the beast, so at first, he only felt the tug on the rope, a sharp pull to the left. Seconds later, there was a burning pain in his arm and he was forced to drop the tether.

Jack looked around. The skid was on its side, most of the coal spilled out over the deck. His fellow Stoker, Matty Stone, who had been pushing the container, was lying beside it. Blood was pooling beneath his head and one hand had vanished beneath the pile of black rocks.

Jack moved quickly around the side of the skid to reach Matty. His feet slipped slightly on the loose coal, but he made it to the man's side.

"Matty! Matty!" he shouted, but he was aware even as he did that his words would be lost in the general din. He shook him, but there was no response. He was, however, still breathing.

Jack looked around. The furnaces were in sight, their heat even now reaching out across the room. Logically, he knew the priority was to get Matty out of the way and to make sure that the coal got to its destination. If the furnace lost heat, it could slow the ship down. Even the loss of that one boiler, out of the 42 in operation, could mean a momentary loss in speed that might cost the ship – and its crew – dearly. But it went against everything he believed to leave the man there.

There was no possibility of a medic getting to them. Even if he could call one from an upper deck, and then if they weren't already busy in the ship's infirmary, getting down to this level of the ship would be hazardous in battle. No one else in the stokehole could help him either. *Do the job you're supposed to, trust in others doing theirs.* To deviate from that was to invite disaster. Jack was on his own.

Quickly, he cleared the coal off his shipmate's hand and arm. It was difficult to see bruising beneath all the coal dust but at least there was no blood. Matty's thumb jutted out at an unusual angle. The unconscious man's sleeve was ripped, and Jack took it and tore a strip off. Gently but quickly, he bound Matty's head where the blood seemed to be coming from, then he hauled his body over to one of the bulkheads and laid him down beside it. Jack crossed the man's arms over his chest, broken thumb uppermost, and hoped that the funereal image it presented was not an omen.

Jack returned to the skid. He crouched down on the floor, braced himself and grasped the lower side with both hands. And lifted. The skid still had some coal in it, so it was even heavier than normal, but still Jack managed to right it. His left hand slipped slightly on the edge of the skid and he looked down to see his sleeve was soaked in blood. Confused, his initial reaction was to wonder if it was Matty's, but then he noticed the slicing cut along the side of his arm, from his elbow to just above his wrist. He knew that it must have happened when the skid went over, but until now adrenaline had stopped him from acknowledging it.

On seeing the wound, however, pain rushed in. There was nothing he could do. Jack pulled his shirt off and wrapped it around the wound, holding one sleeve in his gritted teeth as he tightened the makeshift dressing and tied a knot in it. Then he picked up one of the two shovels that had been in the skid and started to refill it.

Later, after his shift was over, when he'd been relieved and the incoming men – themselves reeling from the battle above – had seen the state he was in, Jack wondered how he had got through the day. For two hours at least, he had filled the skid on his own and pushed it back to the furnaces. A furnace devoured up to one ton of coal in half an hour with the ship at full speed, but his furnace never cooled, never ran short. The Fireman, shovelling coal into the burning kiln and viewing the work through his blue tinted goggles, slowly came to realise that just one man was bringing the fuel to him and worried that he would collapse and the fire would die. But it never happened.

Despite the exhaustion that was clearly written across his body, Jack returned to Matty before he left the stokehole and carried his body up three decks to the infirmary. Matty was still breathing but it was very shallow. His face was covered in coal dust from where he had been lying and with every faint breath out a small cloud of darkness escaped his lips.

Jack knew that someone must have also seen to his arm – field stitches meant he would have a scar in later years – but he didn't remember it.

He didn't realise either that the ship was silent. No guns, no furnace, no shouts even. If he had been more conscious of his surroundings, Jack would have realised that the quiet was not around him but within. He might have worried about the deafness that now wrapped warm arms around him. Instead, he mercifully succumbed to his exhaustion and passed out.

\*\*\*

Three days later, *Lion* returned to Rosyth.

There was no welcoming parade, no cheers. Standing on deck, his arm in a sling and the sounds of the ship only just beginning to return to him, Jack could see people lining the dockside. He didn't need hearing to know they were mourning.

Officially, the action had been a success. The intention had been to engage the German Navy and keep the supply lines open. This had been achieved. Britannia still ruled the waves, but at great cost.

The final figures would be calculated later but a conservative estimate put the British deaths at over 6000 men. Mainly this had been through the loss of several of *Lion*'s sister ships. *HMS Queen Mary* and *HMS Indefatigable* were defeated in the first few minutes of engagement. The sinking of *HMS Invincible* just a few hours later consigned another 1000 souls to the deep. Their loss as *Lion* limped back into harbour was palpable.

Not that Jack needed figures to tell him how it had gone. *Lion* herself had been hit by several shells. Q Gun Turret, situated amidships, had suffered a direct hit and its armoured roof was now blackened and peeled back like some giant sardine tin. One of its great guns stuck up into the air drunkenly. It could have been worse – if the magazines below the turret had caught fire, the ship would have gone, but the fast thinking of Major Francis Harvey, a Marine, in closing all doors and flooding the area saved the ship. It only cost him his life and those of a hundred other men. Jack wasn't sure if he had met Major Harvey or not, but he was grateful to him and he hoped, if they had met, that he had treated him well.

The other indication of their losses was immediately in front of him. Scores of bodies, wrapped in sheets or cloth, ready to be brought home. There was no room down below to store them and here they could at least be given an honour guard as they sailed into port. Tags attached to the sheets identified each man, but Jack wasn't close enough to make out which one was Matty Stone.

The cranes of Rosyth came into view and Jack thought once more of home. Of how grateful he was to be able to go back to his family when so many others would not. How so many families would not even have bodies to bury, the sea their graveyard now. Swansea was a world away, in more ways than one.

*Lion*'s luck had held. She got home, albeit worse for wear and carrying more sorrow than she had left with. Now Jack needed to do the same.

Examples of the medals Jack would have earned during the war. Top to Bottom: Naval Stokers Medal; British Silver Badge, Royal Navy; WW1 War Medal and Victory Medal.

Although the family no longer have Jack's actual medals, they have memories of seeing all of these in his possession.

Jack outside his boxing booth

# Chapter Five

## 1922

The first punch came in hard and fast and if it had landed fully Jack would have been on his back before the fight had even started. Instead, he turned slightly, aware he couldn't dodge it completely, and the blow only hit him on the shoulder. That was the advantage of having studied your opponent. Very often, they just repeated the same moves.

Jack used the momentum of the punch to bring his own fists around to pummel the other man's rib cage whilst his arm was still raised. The fighter staggered backwards under the blows, shaking sweat and surprise out of his eyes.

The crowd, small as it was, shouted their approval. Jack knew that Gladys was out there somewhere, no doubt watching with a disapproving yet worried gaze, but he couldn't waste a second in trying to see her.

The last time they had been to Neath Fair together, back in their courting days, the boxing booths had been closed by the local council. Time passes and councils change and now there were 5 or 6 rings set up amongst the hullabaloo of the fairground, each offering money to the man from the audience who could best their champion. Jack had already claimed the purse at three different booths and he wasn't even tired yet.

The same could not be said of his opponent. Jack had watched him for half an hour before holding up his hand to be next. The man was good, but he had been fighting more or less continually for over two hours. Of course, the main advantage he had held up to now was that he was sober. Virtually all the men who stepped forward to fight were fuelled by beer and bravado, a dangerous combination in a pub but a stupid one here. They paid their entry fee and squared up against the fighter. Three rounds, they had; three rounds to better the professional. Few made it past two. He usually let them get a couple of punches in, let the crowd think they had a chance, and then delivered the finishing blow just a minute or so later. Usually, once down, they stayed down.

Jack, however, was different, and the boxer had realised it from the moment he'd stepped into the ring. Jack's size was usually the intimidating thing about him, but the boxer had bettered men as big as him before. No, the difference here was the calmness that Jack brought with him, a stillness that went beyond sobriety and radiated an absolute surety that he would win. It was unnerving.

The boxer stepped forward again, light on his feet, aware that his main advantage in this fight was probably his speed. Both men were stripped to the waist and Jack was visibly the older of the two. His hair was thinning. There was a long scar on his left arm and the way he moved carried with it the legacy of manual work - aching muscles and a certain slowness. The boxer was young and fit and had never been beaten by an amateur before. There was no need for him to worry.

Two seconds later, the boxer was on his back and the 'referee' – his father and owner of the boxing booth – was stepping forward to hoist Jack's arm up in triumph. He hadn't seen the punch coming at all. It was like a bolt of lightning, Hercules slaying the Nemean lion.

Jack freed himself from the referee and held out a hand to the young man.

"No hard feelings, lad", he said.

The boxer took the offered hand and stood up to cheers from the crowd. He looked at Jack.

"Don't worry," the big man said with a smile. "Now they think you can be beat, they'll be queueing to have a go. You'll make a fortune this afternoon."

Jack turned back to the crowd and held out a hand to the referee. He wanted paying now, with witnesses. The last time he'd agreed to take the payment at the side of the ring, two years previously, the owner had tried to short-change him. This transaction needed to be seen.

The referee paid up and Jack lifted the purse to show the crowd. There were more cheers.

After shaking hands with the boxer and his father, Jack stepped out of the booth. The outside of the attraction was far grander than the interior. The gaily painted frontage proclaimed that 'Championship Fighters' awaited within. Grandly curlicued letters shouted that here was Timpson's Boxing Arena. Paintings of fit, muscular men adorned the boards. Sometimes they were in fighting poses, sometimes they were standing naked (their modesty preserved by a signwriters flourish) in strongman poses. Very few of them resembled the individuals inside. The backgrounds to these pictures were a riot of red and gold, curls and decoration. It was a beautiful sight, but once you had paid your entrance fee and stepped through the curtain at the side, the punter was effectively in a small tent, the ring at its centre no more than a square marked out on the hard ground with rope and corner posts.

Gladys was already waiting for him, over by a booth advertising *The Transparent Lady (See A Good Looking Young Lady Reduced To A Skeleton Via Electrical Appliances!)*

"That was quick," she said, smiling. "Given how long we stayed in there watching first."

"I wanted to see his moves. And anyway, it paid off, didn't it?"

Gladys had to concede the point. "How much did you win?"

Jack handed the money over to her. "A sovereign."

"Grand," his wife exclaimed. "I may not approve of the methods, but I can't argue with the results."

"You know there's no need to worry about me," Jack said. "I've not lost a fight yet." There was a sly smile in his eyes and Gladys knew better than to pursue the matter, noting that even he had used the word 'yet'.

To be fair, Gladys couldn't begrudge her husband this outlet. Since his return from the war, Jack had seemed adrift in civilian life. He'd been lucky in that he had a job to return to at the docks, and – even though he had been invalided out of the navy with 'chronic hearing problems' – he was still physically capable of doing it. Gladys knew of far too many families who had lost fathers, brothers or sons to the conflict or to the injuries that they returned with. Swansea docks was flourishing – the newly named Queens Dock was now open and the creation of the Llandarcy Oil Refinery a few years earlier had brought tankers and new trade to it. In many ways, they were very lucky. They finally even had a house of their own, although it felt like Jack's parents spent more time there than in their own home.

Yet still something was missing from Jack's life. At first, she thought it was the camaraderie of the navy, but eventually Gladys realised what he needed was the opportunity to show off. Not that Jack was a vain man, far from it, but something from his Music Hall days had gotten into his blood. Perhaps it had always been there, discovered in his earliest shows on the Sands but amplified by the stage. Whatever the cause, he was happiest with an audience – be that his children or his dock mates or a group of rowdy drunkards baying for blood in a small tent.

The Music Hall, however, was gone. Physically, the old Palace building was now purely a cinema, one of a chain that Billy Coutts now owned and ran. The Coutts Organisation, as it was grandly called, employed nearly 200 people and ran 10 cinemas. Billy had gone from a small-time manager to a fully-fledged impresario, but in moving with the times he also sounded the death knell for acts like The Welsh Hercules. He still brought one-off spectaculars to Swansea – a Buffalo Bill Wild West Show and the demonstrations of Dr Walford Bodie (whose acts of 'bloodless surgery' healed the lame on stage through electrocution) had both done very well for him – but turns like Jack were now distinctly small fry.

So, if the annual Neath Fair gave him the opportunity to shine in front of an audience again - and to make some money along the way - who was she to complain? With a growing family, they could certainly use every penny they could get.

\*\*\*

The old man swore in Greek. Gladys recognised the word but had never asked her husband or her mother-in-law to translate it. Some things were better left unknown.

Despite being almost 80 years old, Giovani Snr still had some fight left in him. Unfortunately, and especially now that he was no longer working, that fight was usually with his eldest son. Today, however, an argument had been expected.

"You cannot just leave your job and run away with the Fairground!" Giovani Snr bellowed. "Think of your family!"

Gladys wished her father-in-law would think of their family a little too – his shouting had awoken baby Leslie and little two-year old Dorothy was clinging to her leg in fear. All the older children had a fear of their grandfather, of his tempers and his stern ways. It looked like the youngest would learn that fear first-hand too. Jack Jnr, at only six years of age, already knew to take his younger sisters into the other room when the volume reached a certain level and now he crept forward to take Dorothy away from the argument. The two eldest girls, Lily and Winnifred, had already gone outside to play in the street.

Jack wasn't going to raise his voice in response, but his blood was boiling nonetheless. He had meant this to be a family discussion – *his* family, not including the older generation. He knew what he wanted the outcome to be, but he wanted to talk to all of them about it. It was a big change, especially for Gladys.

"I'm not running away anywhere," he said carefully. "And the reason I'm doing it is *for* my family."

The old man spat on the ground. "You are doing this for yourself. So that people can come and smile at you again and clap for you and shout your name. *My* name! You are doing this to show off."

Not for the first time, Gladys reflected that Giovani Snr was able to anger his son so easily precisely because he knew exactly which areas to attack. The ones that had a glimmer of truth in them.

"And how is this any different than you leaving your family for weeks at a time on the *Prestonian*? This way, I can bring in more money in one week at the fairground than I could make in a fortnight at the docks," Jack said. He declined to add that it would amount to more money than the old man brought back for the same period away as well. That would be too provoking – and, besides, Jack knew it only applied if the fair was busy and he attracted enough customers. That was an argument for another day, though.

If he was honest about it, there were a lot of elements about what he was suggesting that were problematic, but he wasn't about to share them with his father.

The proposal had come shortly after he had bested the boxer in Timpson's booth. Gladys had gone off to find some small trinkets or toys to take back for the girls – they had wanted to come along but Gladys knew that she couldn't keep an eye on them and Jack at the same time, so they had ended up staying at home. Jack was setting off in search of the next boxing booth when he felt a firm hand on his arm.

"Excuse me, friend," a deep voice said. "I wonder if I could have a word."

Jack turned to see a man of medium height and build wearing a loud houndstooth suit. His hair was starting to grey, but it was brushed neatly back and secured in position with pomade. He looked vaguely familiar.

"Taylor's the name," the man said, sticking his hand out to shake. "You may have seen me around. Mine was the second booth you won in."

Confused, Jack shook the offered hand and introduced himself in turn.

"You're a good fighter," Taylor continued. "Did you box in the army?"

"Navy," Jack corrected. "When I wasn't playing rugby."

"Thought so, thought so," Taylor nodded. "And you saw action too. That scar on your arm?"

Unconsciously, Jack glanced down at his forearm. "Jutland."

Taylor nodded some more. "One of the ships that didn't go wrong," he said. Jack knew what he was referring to – Vice Admiral Beatty's widely-reported, and widely hated, comment about how the loss of two thousand lives was because 'there seems to be something wrong with our bloody ships today'. From anybody else, it would have seemed like a flippant comment, something to anger Jack, but the man before him said it with a deep sorrow in his voice.

"I was on *Lion*. Did you have family on some of the ships that went down?"

Taylor shook his head. "Not family. Friends. As good as family."

The two men were quiet for a moment, a stillness holding them in the midst of the gaudy fairground.

"But I'm not here to reminisce," Taylor suddenly said, and clapped Jack on the back. "Will you join me in a drink?"

"I'd rather know why you want to drink with me first," Jack replied.

Taylor threw his head back and gave a short barking laugh. "Good man! Good man! The beer tent is this way!" He strode off in the direction he'd indicated without waiting to see if Jack was following.

Jack considered for a moment and then set off after him. He had to admit to being intrigued.

By the time he reached him in the beer tent, Taylor was already ordering two pints.

"Sarsaparilla for me," Jack corrected. The other man looked at him in surprise but recovered quickly and changed the order.

"Religious type?" Taylor asked, nodding towards the soft drink.

"No more than any other Welshman," Jack smiled. "I go to church when I can, but I don't worry if I can't. The temperance is just because I like to be the one in control of my body, not some bottle."

Taylor nodded and they took a seat at a small wooden table in a corner. Nowhere in the beer tent could be described as quiet, but this was at least away from the general hullabaloo of the bar.

"I'd like to offer you a job," said Taylor. "I saw you in my boxing booth and then followed you to the others and you're a natural fighter, that much is obvious. I daresay you'd been doing it before the Navy too and they just refined your skills a bit. You have moves that I've only seen in a pro."

Jack wiped his mouth. "Thank you. But I'm not interested in just being a fighter all my life. It's a nice diversion, but I've got a family to think about."

"And I wouldn't waste your talents on just fighting, either," Taylor replied. "Do you know what I am?" He didn't give Jack time to answer. "I'm what we call a Showman. From a family of Showmen, several generations back. You work in the fairgrounds, the circuses, you live that life – you're a Showman.

"It's about grift, and hard work, and just a bit of a flair for the theatrical. And I see it in you. You, Jack, have the makings of a Showman."

"Well, I used to be on stage," Jack said. "At the Palace in Swansea."

"I knew it!", Taylor cried out, clapping his hands together as he did. "I knew it. The way you worked those crowds, even as the newcomer – a punter! - you knew what you were doing!"

Jack explained about his time as The Welsh Hercules and Taylor nodded enthusiastically throughout. At the end of his story, Jack took a swig of his largely-untouched sarsaparilla and noted that Taylor was already draining his own glass.

The Showman slammed the empty glass down on the table. "So," he said, "Let's get down to business. I want to offer you the chance of a lifetime."

And then had come the offer. Taylor – never Mr Taylor, and certainly never referred to by his first name, Charlie – had an attraction that he needed a manager for. A Wall of Death sideshow. The previous manager had moved on, got his own attraction, and now the whole thing was in Taylor's winter storage. The way Taylor described it, Jack would run and maintain the Wall inside the tent, with Taylor (at least initially) providing the motorcycle riders. Anything that happened outside the tent to attract customers, was completely down to Jack. If he wanted to do a Strongman act, he could; if he wanted to hone his patter when talking to an audience, here was the chance. Whatever he did, it was Jack's responsibility to get people to pay up and walk through that curtain, and if he did that he would get a split of the take with Taylor.

"Sixty - Forty split," Taylor explained. "In my favour."

"How about we reverse that and I get the Sixty?" Jack said.

"Oh now, don't be pushing your luck," Taylor smiled. "I'm providing the attraction, all the equipment, the riders, and I'll stand you the ground rent at the fairs for the first 6 months. I'll even find you a second person to put your name forward for membership of the Showman's Guild. I think that's a good deal."

"True," said Jack. "But I have a family to think of and a steady source of income to give up. Plus, I'll be travelling away from home for long periods. As I see it, I'm helping you more than you're helping me. Your Wall is earning nothing at the moment. In fact, it's probably in need of maintenance and will need more the longer it's out of use. I could walk away and still have a good job - but you'd still have an attraction rotting in storage and not earning a penny.

"And let's not forget it's in your interest to get me into the Guild, because without that membership I can't run your attraction."

For a moment, Jack wondered if he had pushed too hard, but Taylor surprised him. The barking laugh returned along with a broad and genuine grin.

"I knew you were a bloody Showman," Taylor said. "Sixty – Forty to you. But you pay your own ground rent. Take it or leave it."

In the end, Jack took it, on the proviso that he discussed it with his family first. He'd wondered if that might have been a deal-breaker, but Taylor was a family man too and was quite pleased to see that Jack was also anchored in that way. All of which had led back, later that same night, to the current argument with his father.

"It doesn't matter what I say," Giovani Snr snarled. "You will do what you want. Always have. You never listen to your father."

"Not when he's spouting rubbish, I don't!" Jack replied. The look his father gave him made him regret being so forthright, but the time for subtlety with the old man was long gone. "And if your precious name is what is really bothering you, I'll change it. God forbid anyone should connect a successful family man with you!"

The days of Giovani Snr being able to storm out of a room were long gone. Arthritis had slowed him down and he now walked with a stick. But the stick had become his greatest weapon. He could use it as a prod or to clip a grandchild if he thought they were misbehaving. It could be waved in the air to emphasise a point. Or he could slam it down on the ground, as he did now, to show his displeasure.

"I will not stay in a house that does not respect me!" he said, using the stick to draw himself up from his seat. Gladys took a step forward to help him but he shot her a glance that stopped her in her tracks.

"If you take this... job," he spat out the word, "you will never see me in this house again. You will not drag the Lamnea name down. I told you when you were prancing about on the stage that it was no work for a man, but even that was better than abandoning your family to run around the country posing!"

The old man turned his back to leave, but Jack needed to say more.

"Would you rather I ran myself into the ground here for them? Worked myself into a cripple like you? Or would you rather have me fall prey to an accident like Gwyn Arthur, God rest his soul? This is a way of giving everyone a better life, even me. Why can't you see that?"

Giovani Snr did not look round as he spoke. "A father sacrifices. A father works for his family, not for his own glory. The only good work you have ever done was on that ship. Sometimes, I wish you had stayed there. Or in the sea surrounding it."

The old man pulled open the door and stepped out into the outside world, leaving Jack ashen-faced behind him.

Jack, on the floor, lifting Pat Collins, Winnie Davies, and Kaison Bates.

Lily and Winnie, Jack Lamnea's daughters, both boxers.

From an article in World's Fair Newspaper,
2008

# Chapter Six

## 1928

The bus needed a lot of work.

It had been all over the country with its current owners and had taken quite a punishing as a result, but Jack could see the potential in it. He'd need to take out all the seats, black out the windows. Some form of roof rack would need to be made to carry the poles for the booth. The interior would need to be entirely gutted and then sectioned up to create living quarters and storage areas. It wouldn't be easy, but it would be worth it.

"Of course, it's in Foden's interest to keep her in good nick," the man in front of him was saying. "Wouldn't look good for the band bearing their name to break down somewhere on the way to a gig, now, would it?"

Jack nodded. It had been pure coincidence that he'd seen the bus. He was at the Codona Family's Spring Holiday Fair in Aberdeen. The Codona's were virtual Showman Royalty – of Italian descent, they were originally a circus family, but their canny business acumen had since seen them make the jump to cinemas and then to steam-driven fairground rides. Jack knew of the Codona

patriarch, Alfred, although he had never met him –
all of his dealings had been with his sons, William,
Frank, John and Nathaniel. Most of the rides at the
Spring Fair were owned by the family, with the
Galloping Horses calliope, Cake Walk and Switch
Back all situated proudly in the centre of the
grounds at Kittybrewster Mart while the lesser
attractions (and rented spaces) crowded around the
edges. The Codona's also owned Fun City outside
Edinburgh, Scotland's first permanent Amusement
Park, so, as a result, it was quite an honour to be
part of their Spring Fair. Although it had cost Jack
more than usual to get a pitch, it was worth it for
the hundreds of punters who would pass by him
daily.

In a bid to attract even more customers,
however, the Codona's had also hired the most
famous band in the UK to appear at the fairgrounds
– The Foden Motor Works Brass Band. It was rare
for them to stray outside the North West or
London, but a nearby competition had tempted
them across the border and the Codona's had taken
advantage of it. Posters all around the fairground
announced the free concert by the British Open
Champions and punters had flooded in as a result.
The concert was later in the day, but meanwhile
Jack had taken the opportunity to go over and see
what the fuss was about. The bandsmen and their
conductor had all gone into town, though, leaving

just the official Foden's driver and the most beautiful bus Jack had ever seen. A bus, it transpired, that was soon to be replaced and was therefore up for sale...

Jack shivered slightly. He was wearing his show costume – white leggings under a dark red leotard trimmed with gold and cut across the chest to show his physique – under a rain coat. At that point, Aberdeen was the furthest North Jack had ever been and he was starting to wonder if the Scots had a different definition of Spring to the rest of the country. The wind coming off the sea was bracing, and the sky had stayed slate grey for the three days he'd been there so far, matching the sombre pallor of the city's granite buildings. But the dour Scottish atmosphere was completely banished as soon as you arrived at the Fairground's site. Steam organs played jauntily strident versions of popular songs like *The Good Old Bad Old Days* and even *Waltzing Mathilda*, and the shadows of punters swayed merrily in time to the music as the wind caught the electric lights strung from booth to booth. Some booths still used naphtha flare lamps as illumination, preferring the warmth of the tilly lamp's light over electricity, and Jack had to admit that he quite liked catching the smell of them on the breeze occasionally. It was a proper fairground smell in his mind, mixed in with the sweetness of toffee apples and the oil of the traction engines.

He smiled at how quickly he had taken to the Showman's world. Following his conversation with Taylor all those years ago, Jack had paid his first annual 4 shilling fee and been accepted into the Welsh Section of the Showman's Guild in 1923. By doing so, he had taken on the responsibility for running a booth under the regulations of the Guild and had gained permission to operate on any fairground in the country. It was a bold new move for him and (thankfully) one which Gladys had supported. To mark it, he had also taken on a new name and was now known, on documents and on the front of his booth, as Jack Lemm. Whether this had been done to appease his father or to anger him, Jack was never sure, and as the old man, true to his word, had never stepped foot in Jack's house after that fateful argument, he had not had the chance to see how it had been received. Whatever the reasoning, it wasn't too far from his real name to feel alien to him – and it didn't hurt that it sounded very like John Lemm, a world-famous strongman from Switzerland. Jack had grinned when he first wrote his new name - evidently, all those years with Billy Coutts had rubbed off on him.

Having started with Taylor's Wall of Death, Jack had built up his own act to the extent that, three years ago, he had been able to make the split from his mentor and go his own way. At first, he thought Taylor would have been upset at him handing the attraction back, but it seemed the shrewd Showman had been expecting it. "Surprised it took you so long," he said. Indeed, Taylor already had someone else in line to take over the Wall and he knew he was getting an attraction back that was in much better condition than it had been when Jack took it on, so all in all he was not overly concerned about the situation.

Jack, meanwhile, had grown and blossomed in the fairground world. The Front Act, the part of the show performed for free outside the booth to attract customers, had been his making. Given free reign, Jack had managed to work on his strongman act alongside developing his patter, somehow managing to combine the two diverse parts of his attraction in the minds of his audience and getting them to pay up to see the rest. After a while, he had even taken on a second act to help with the load. Billy Warren was a strongman too, but his was a much more gymnastic strength. He was very nimble and was able to do crowd-pleasing back flips and leaps, and the fact that he was a smaller man with a slimmer body made Jack's physique stand out all the more. They shared the load with the patter, Jack bringing the young showman up in the same sort of way that Billy Coutts had with him, and for a while they were one of the main attractions at whichever fair they travelled to.

When Jack gave back the Wall of Death, however, it gave him the chance to expand his own act even further. Having saved enough to have his own booth now, he launched *Jack Lemm And His Famous Troupe of First Class Athletes and Boxers*, additionally billing himself as *The Wonder Man – Direct From the Leading Music Halls of Great Britain*. Alongside Billy Warren, Jack also took on another apprentice strongman, Arthur Brown, who could be billed as a Champion Boxer as well. Having enticed the punter into his tent, Jack was now able to provide a full show of gymnastics, feats of strength and boxing – and he continued the tradition that started him off by including bouts against members of the audience.

By the time he reached Aberdeen, Jack Lemm's Troupe were putting on a punishing 40 shows a day, from 11am to 11pm. The content of the shows varied to allow different members of the troupe to take a break, but the biggest saving grace had been when Jack had realised that he didn't need to supply the boxers – he just needed to provide a ring. Quite often when he'd asked for a member of the audience to come forward to fight, two or more men would have stepped up together, intending to use their prowess in the ring to prove who was the better fighter. The obvious solution, Jack soon realised, was to just put the two men in the square together and have them beat the living daylights out of each other. The crowds loved it, the participants wanted it, and Jack and his fighters got to step back briefly and take a breather. He didn't even need to pay prize money to the victor.

If he was honest with himself, Jack was loving his new life. Yes, it kept him away from home for large periods of time, but it allowed him to travel the country and to meet new people, to see places he never thought he would get the chance to see. His troupe, though small, were fiercely loyal to him and the showmen he met at different fairs were all good hard-working folk. It was a community – one where some groups travelled together and others orbited them, meeting up again at the same events year after year, immediately falling back into conversations or disputes that had been started months before. There was something very comforting about it.

Gladys occasionally came out to see him or to stay for a few days when her work, and geography, allowed. She never complained about his being away so much but he could see from the joy in her eyes when they met that she missed him. When they parted, they both felt the sharp prick of tears, although Jack rarely let it show.

Jack always presented a stoical attitude about their separation, but in truth it hurt him too. He was missing the children growing up, missing time with the woman he loved, but he consoled himself with the thought that he was providing for all of them. Occasionally, he would manage to get home to see everyone, or to take Gladys out for a day (like the tram ride to Mumbles they had enjoyed the previous autumn), but these visits were rare.

As for the children, all of them came to visit whenever their father worked Neath, Cardiff or Swansea fair, their exuberant joy and wide-eyed excitement reigniting his love for this new life. That enthusiasm, however, had proved especially attractive to one member of his family – his daughter, Winnie, had been travelling with him for the last year.

His eldest daughter, Lily, had also travelled with them for a while but in the end the nomadic lifestyle had not been for her. Jack couldn't blame her, but the two girls had always been chalk to the other's cheese so it came as no surprise to him when Winnie had proved herself to be a very able part of Jack's troupe. Although she appeared under the name Winnie Davies (something which no-one queried, given her Welsh accent), she was every bit her father's daughter.

Her speciality was boxing, although she occasionally helped her Dad out with the props for his strongman act as well. Billed as *The Flyweight*

*Champion Lady Boxer*, Winnie had spent a long time watching Jack and other boxers in the ring before venturing into it herself. She had several advantages on her side: she was light on her feet and could often sidestep the most aggressive opponents, tiring them out before delivering the final blow; she was a woman and therefore her strength was often underestimated by the drunken men she squared up to; and above all, she could actually fight, which generally came as a surprise to those who took her on.

She had started by squaring up to her sister, who performed under the name Lillie Ray. Jack had noticed them play-sparring outside the tent and one day just announced to a crowd, Billy Coutts-style, that two lady boxers would give an exhibition bout a few days later. The two sisters were surprised but being in the glare of the spotlight ran in the family. In the days that followed, Jack coached the two of them, showed them how to pull punches and how to play to the crowd, and then put them in front of an audience. *The Fistic Females* were an immediate success, but when Lily left, Winnie convinced her father to let her box men as well, challenging all-comers in the flyweight and middleweight classes.

So far, Winnie had only been knocked out once – the result of a lucky punch from a burly farm labourer - and she didn't intend for it to happen again.

Jack didn't say it very often, but he was inordinately proud of Winnie. At only 15, she was strong, independent, and earning, not only for herself but for the whole family.

In part, this was the reason why he was looking for a new bus. The converted truck that he lived out of at the moment had been fine when he was starting out in the business. It could carry the booth and all his props, plus provide a modest living space for himself in the form of the 'wee wagon' situated behind the driver's cab, but, truth be told, the vehicle had been old when he'd bought it and now that Winnie was staying with him, he needed more space. They had managed this far, but even Jack couldn't deny his daughter was growing up and needed room to herself.

"So, are you interested or not?"

The man with the bus snapped Jack back out of his reveries.

"Yes, I am," he replied, cautiously. "But she has a lot of miles on her, and I don't think your bandsmen will have treated her kindly. Plus, she'll need a whole new paint job." He rubbed his chin, thoughtfully. "Knock a quarter off and you might have a deal."

Jack knew this was only the opening gambit, but he felt compelled to go in low. She was a beautiful bus, and it would take time and work to make her into a home fit for the road, but he wasn't going to leave without her. It would stretch his budget whatever the outcome - and it would be better if Gladys never knew the full price no matter what the deal.

The owner of the bus was about to answer when the pair were interrupted.

"Dad!", Winnie shouted across from the fairground.

Jack turned to see his daughter running over to him, waving a piece of paper. He apologised to the man and turned to face her.

"What is it, girl? Why the all-fired rush?"

Winnie stopped and caught her breath, holding out the paper towards him. "Telegram."

Jack frowned. He wasn't expecting anything, and, after the war, unexpected telegrams carried with them a certain darkness. He took the paper and opened it. His face was unreadable.

On it were six words.

*Come Home. Your Father Is Dead.*

\*\*\*

The journey home was long and difficult.

Jack had no choice but to leave Winnie in charge of the booth. They couldn't pack up and leave together – monetarily, the loss would be heavy, but Jack also had the other members of his troupe to think of and how they would cope if he had to close, even briefly. And then there was also the practical side of closing down midway through a fair – the inconvenience to the other booths around them, the sheer difficulty of getting all his equipment out of the fairground when it was part of a wall of other booths. No, the show must go on, as they say, and who better than Winnie to look after it?

That said, Jack had still gone to William Codona, the eldest of the Codona brothers and lessee for the fair, to explain his absence. Partly this was just common courtesy, as William was overseeing everything about the fair for his family, but also Jack wanted to know that someone there would be keeping an eye out for Winnie in his absence. He had known William for about two years and the two got on well. It had been at William's invitation that Jack had come to Aberdeen as, between them, the four Codona brothers ran most of Scotland's fairground scene. Jack knew Winnie was capable of running the booth in his absence, but he was also painfully aware that she was still young and that young women were the source of a lot of attention from young males, both within the Showman community and without. If it was known that William was watching over her, it would deter a lot of advances.

Even so, the wild card in this scenario was Winnie herself. She was as headstrong as her father and if she wanted to meet up with a boy, she'd find a way. Knowing this, Jack had been determined to have a stern talk with her before leaving. In particular, he had warned her off the Blockley boy who had been sniffing around since their visit to Kirkcaldy Links Market Fair a week earlier. His family owned the largest Slip - the Showman's term for a Helter Skelter - on that fairground and Winnie and he had apparently hit it off.

When the Blockleys had then moved on to the Aberdeen fair as well, he'd noticed Winnie had perked up considerably and he couldn't help feeling the two of them were probably planning something, even before the news from home took Jack out of the picture. Jack couldn't say why, but he really wasn't keen on the Blockley boy. It was nothing that he'd done – he just didn't trust him as far as he could throw him (which in Jack's case was a pretty redundant phrase as he could probably throw the kid a good distance without breaking a sweat). At least, with Winnie left in charge of the booth, the opportunities for the two to get together would be more limited.

Jack was also unable to drive home as the truck was needed at the fairground, so he'd been forced to go by rail. It was not a means of transport he enjoyed – sitting for long periods of time was against his nature – but it was a necessary evil. Even so, it took an age. From Aberdeen, he travelled to Manchester. There he discovered that his next train wouldn't leave until the morning, so begrudgingly Jack accepted he would have to spend the night in the northern city. He couldn't afford a hotel, and the thought of a Salvation Army hostel brought back memories of the awful conditions and violent atmosphere of his days at *HMS Vivid*, so instead he resigned himself to spending the night on a bench in Piccadilly Gardens. It was cold, but not as cold as Aberdeen, and there was no trouble once the local prostitutes realised he wasn't interested in their wares. All the same, he spent most of the night cursing his father for having forced him into this journey.

From Manchester, the next train was to Birmingham, then from there to Newport and –

finally! - on to Swansea. Jack arrived, tired and hungry, just as the sun was setting. No one was there to greet him.

*\*\*\**

The chair by the fireplace was empty. Although he had known it would be, Jack still found himself surprised to see it. The absence of his father filled the room.

The crossed swords still glinted over the fireplace, catching the little light coming from the grate. All the curtains were closed and would remain that way until after the funeral, a mark of respect and an outward show to the world that death had visited the house. A gas lamp flickered slightly and shadows jumped in the corners of the kitchen.

Jack had come to the house alone. Gladys had taken his mother in at their own home and, although evidently upset, Rovena seemed comforted to have the life of a family around her. Jack had spent an hour or so with her there before coming to his parent's house. The house he had grown up in. Grown out of. He came not because he particularly wanted to but because his mother had insisted. And now that he was here, he wasn't sure why he needed to be.

Jack found himself glancing over to the back door, as if expecting it to open suddenly and for his father to stride in from the privy. Not that his father had been able to stride anywhere for a long time. First he had walked with the stick; then later, as the arthritis took over, he seemed to force himself to move through sheer will power and bloody-mindedness.

The old man had died in bed, Jack knew that. No reason seemed necessary – his heart had just finally stopped at the age of 85. Luckily, his mother had not woken to find him that way. She had been downstairs, preparing the breakfast when he passed. She told Jack that they had woken up together and kissed each other good morning before she departed. That little detail was the strangest thing to Jack. He had never seen his parents kiss, never spotted a tender moment between them. It suggested a whole parallel life that he had somehow missed, a side to his parents that could have changed his whole outlook on them.

There was no point in his hanging around in the kitchen and thinking of these things, though. The reason for his visit lay in the Front Room, the parlour, the room he and his siblings had hardly been allowed into when they were children. His mother had always kept the parlour immaculate, 'in case we have guests'. The mythical guests, or at least any important enough to be given admittance to the room, never arrived but the parlour stayed pristine in anticipation of them. Now it held a dignitary of a different type.

The coffin took up the centre of the room, all the furniture within it having been pushed back towards the walls. Again, the curtains were closed and only the lamp that Jack had brought through from the kitchen provided any light.

Jack stood on the threshold of the room for a minute, taking it in. The casket was open. This was important in his father's Greek Orthodox religion but not unusual in itself. Too many people worried about premature burial, of waking to find themselves trapped in a box beneath the ground, so now the tradition of lying in state this way almost bypassed religious concerns. There was a faintly sweet, faintly sickly smell to the room.

Jack stepped forward and looked down at the body.

It wasn't his father. It was a good facsimile, but the body was too small, the skin stretched too much over the face. His father had always been animated by a spark – of indignation, of anger, of spite – something that gave him his defining features. The way he turned his head, the angle of his shoulders when he sat. Lying here, totally still, with his arms crossed over his chest and in a room Jack had never really seen him in, the body looked like a marionette whose strings had been cut. He couldn't connect it with the man he had known.

But suddenly, he found himself wishing that he had known this man instead. A peaceful man. A man who didn't feel he'd had to fight for everything in his life. Or fight against everything in his life. This man in his best suit, he now understood, was who his mother saw. Who she had originally fallen for. It was the man underneath all the concerns for his family, for the family name, for the future of his children.

It was a man, Jack realised, that he had actively pushed away.

The tears flowed down Jack's face before he'd even known he was crying. He put a hand out and steadied himself on the coffin. Memories were flooding back – of arguments and fights, harsh words spoken – and buried deep beneath them, just a flicker of recollection, of his father smiling at him, of a proud man watching his son play with a boat on a stream. A man that looked more like the one before him.

Jack lifted his hand to wipe his eyes and a sharp sting stopped him. He looked down at his hand. A splinter was sticking out of one finger. Gently, Jack pulled it out and looked at the small bubble of blood that appeared in its place.

Jack looked at the casket and chuckled.

"You always did want the last word, you old bastard."

A few moments later, still chuckling, Jack left the house of his youth and stepped out into the cold Swansea night.

Jack and his son, Jack Jnr.

# Chapter Seven

**February 19<sup>th</sup>, 1941**

"Lead with your left!"

Jack watched as the young boy in front of him hesitated for a moment in the ring. He saw the slight shake of his right hand and knew the lad was mimicking holding a pen inside his boxing glove. It was that momentary distraction that proved his undoing. Before he had processed which hand he was being told to lead with, his opponent had landed a punch and the fight was over.

Jack nodded at the young lad in the corner of the ring and the bell rang out to signal the end of the bout. The losing fighter was starting to pick himself up off the canvas, and Jack swung up through the ropes and held out a hand to him.

"C'mon, Teddy," he said. "You'll do better next time."

Edward Lamnea, ten years old and already aware that he would never be a fighter, looked up at his father and bit back the tears that were welling up in him. It wasn't that the punch had particularly hurt (although there would be a bruise) or that he had let his father down, just that there was the prospect of a 'next time'. Boxing was his father's world and, although he enjoyed this time with him, it was not a profession he intended to follow. Teddy was much more interested in being a train driver and he was pretty sure that did not involve punching anyone very often.

All the same, the young lad accepted his father's hand and stood up. Jack gave him a playful cuff on the back of his head. "Go have a wash," he said.

As Teddy jumped down from the ring and two other lads prepared to take his place, Jack reflected briefly on his son's performance. He knew that it was tough for the boy – his older brothers, Jack and Leslie, were away fighting in the Army and this left the young Edward at home in a sea of women. Mother, sisters, aunties all swirled around him, the war having taken most of the men in his life. Lacking sibling rivalry, Edward, like many of the young lads in the area, needed something to take his aggression out on, even if he himself didn't realise it, and Jack had decided boxing was the perfect solution.

Of course, Jack had wanted to fight in the War himself but, to his annoyance, he had not been allowed to. Being 52 years old wasn't the problem (when he'd tried signing up, the doctor had been visibly impressed by his physique and general state of health), rather the fact that he had been invalided out of the Navy proved to be the sticking point. A fact that Jack could hardly deny when his hearing tests classified him as virtually deaf.

If he was honest with himself, Jack knew his hearing had deteriorated over the years since Jutland, but he didn't let it get the better of him. So, sounds were a little duller, voices not as clear. You spoke up in his presence or you didn't have anything to say. It was that easy.

All the boys in the Swansea Invictus Club knew Mr Lamnea was hard of hearing and, at first, this looked like the perfect excuse to misbehave when he was around. They soon realised, however, that although his hearing was dim, his wits were sharp – and he was not above clipping any of them around the ear if he caught them up to mischief.

Not that they would have got up to a lot in his presence. Jack was a local celebrity, still famed for his Music Hall years and well-known for his strongman act at local fairs. He was the kind of man their fathers had talked about before they had gone away and that their grandfathers knew of still. Stories of Jack felling three men in one fight, or breaking records in the ring, flew around the boxing club and Jack allowed all of them to stand, whether they were true or not.

Jack enjoyed his time at the Invictus. He'd coached there before but travelling with the fairs meant it had only been an occasional thing. Now he was able to give three nights a week to it and the prospect of using their gym also meant he was often around even when not coaching. Still, he missed the fairs – he knew that some cities like Cardiff and Birmingham had managed to keep some rides and booths going by moving everything indoors or only operating in daylight hours, but the places at these grounds were hard to come by and, besides, most of his troupe were away fighting. He could have appeared on his own, but he'd gotten used to running a group of artists, enjoying the camaraderie of the road.

The Showman's Guild was still part of his life, though, and his boxing matches helped to raise cash towards the Spitfire fund they had initiated.

In all, despite not being able to fight abroad, Jack counted himself lucky. He had his family around him, he had an outlet for his boxing and exercises in the Invictus Club, and he had a steady income, having returned to the docks as soon as he got home. He was still doing his bit for the war effort. Dockyard working, like the railway next to it, was a protected industry, so theoretically there should not have been as much need for him, but although dockers over 30 were spared conscription, a lot of men had left and signed up anyway. The resulting workplace was a little strange to him – there were no young men around and some jobs had even been taken over by women – but there would always be a need for someone with his strength and experience.

The bell rang for the next bout to begin. Tommy Whitaker was sizing up against Geraint Arthur. The latter lad was huge for his age, an oxen amongst cattle, but his movements were slow and he tired quickly in the ring. Jack knew that Geraint's first love was rugby and he could see a future for him there as an immovable prop. Meanwhile, if the Whitaker boy could just ride the match out, he could walk away like David after defeating Goliath.

Jack looked around to see where Teddy was. The boy had finished washing and was now getting dressed ready to go back home. He sat on a bench, tying his shoelaces next to a battered punch bag. Jack noted that some local wag had drawn a caricature of Hitler's face over the most heavily beaten part of the bag.

He smiled and, as he turned his attention back to the ring, a single bright flare of light caught his eye. It was from one of the windows, where there was a tear in the brown paper pasted over them to keep the light from spilling out. At the same time, he saw a couple of the boys looking up, nervously.

"Is it a fizzer?" one of them asked.

"Stay here!" Jack barked and rushed over to the front door of the club. He opened it and immediately the sound of the Air Raid siren filled the room. Outside there was another bright flash to his left.

"Everybody to me! Now!" Jack shouted as he closed the door again.

Boys scrambled from all sides of the room. One ran the other way to get his shoes and Jack bellowed for him to leave them. Within seconds, all the boys were gathered around him. Teddy was in the middle of them, looking scared but determined.

"Right, lads, we are going to go to the public shelter on the Strand. It's only five minutes away. We can –" Jack was cut short by the looks on the children's faces.

They could hear something he couldn't. A fizzer, as it was known, was an incendiary bomb. It didn't explode on impact, but the force of landing set off a small charge inside it which ignited a thermite filling causing a very hot, very destructive fire. Very often you would not hear the device drop, so the only giveaway was the sound of the chemical reaction fizzing, hence the nickname. Unfortunately, if you could hear that, you were probably too close for safety.

"I can hear it! It's upstairs!" Tommy Whitaker shouted and pointed up at the ceiling.

Jack knew it was possible for a device to have fallen on the building but still fail to have penetrated more than one floor. In themselves, fizzers didn't do a lot of damage. If you could douse one in water before the charge went off, you could even stop the fire from happening. But if they ignited whilst lodged in a roof or a floor, they could lead to the whole building burning down. Jack couldn't hear anything except the wail of the sirens, but the looks of panic on the boys' faces meant he had to get them out of the building - even if he was just dealing with an overactive imagination.

"Look at me!" he yelled, and the hubbub quelled. "We are getting out of here. But we need to stay together. Everybody watch out for everyone else. Now follow me."

He opened the door and stepped out onto the darkened street. Behind one of the buildings opposite him, Jack could see the faint glow of a fire burning. The night sky was streaked with floodlights and the bright scratches of anti-aircraft guns. He could dimly make out the sound of people shouting, the sound muffled by the pounding of the AA guns and, beneath all of it, the undulating hum of German planes overhead.

"This way," he shouted and gestured up the road. The boys set off as Jack waited to make sure that everybody was out of the building. He was suddenly aware of how cold it was.

Abruptly, the whole street was lit up by an unnaturally bright light. Jack's first thought was that something nearby must have exploded, but there was no new noise. Looking up, he realised what it was. A flare. Dropped by the Luftwaffe to illuminate the area they were to attack. This, he realised, must have been what he first saw through the window of the Invictus Club.

As the flare went off, the boys stopped in the street as if transfixed. They stared at each other in complete terror, suddenly exposed. Jack slammed the Club door shut behind him and yelled at them once again. "No lollygagging! Get going!"

His voice shocked them into movement. Jack was momentarily relieved. He knew that if the planes were lighting up an area, they were just about to drop more bombs on it, and he needed the boys to run.

They had just reached the end of the street when the next wave of incendiary bombs fell. Jack stopped the boys and told them to flatten themselves against a nearby wall. He wasn't sure what good it would do but it seemed like the only option. He could see the entrance to the public shelter just a few yards away, but he dared not try to reach it. As if reading his thoughts, an Air Raid Warden appeared from within the shelter and beckoned to him to stay where he was.

The bombs came down. Mostly Jack was only aware of them if they hit something, the crunch of impact followed by masonry hitting the street or the sound of wood splintering. Occasionally, one was visible as it fell, thrown into a sudden silhouette by a sister device bursting into fiery life. All around them, bright eyes of flame winked open behind windows or peeked out through damaged walls. And still the noise of the attack continued to deafen them.

Suddenly, with a surprisingly harsh clatter, something dropped to the ground in front of the boys. Everybody stared at the object and Jack could see that it was a cylindrical tube with metal fins on one end. A fizzer. It was impossible to tell in the commotion around them if it was making a noise or not, but Jack knew he had to get the boys away from it no matter what. He was just stepping away from the wall to tell them to run when Geraint Arthur took a step forward and performed a perfect drop kick on the bomb. It sailed up and away from the group and disappeared through the broken window of a shop across the street. Geraint winked at him and then took his place against the wall once again.

Jack wasn't sure if that was the bravest or the stupidest thing he had ever seen, but he wasted no time in using the moment it gave them.

"Run!" he shouted, and everyone raced for the shelter.

*＊＊

"You're mad if you go out there again!"

The Air Raid Warden knew that he couldn't physically stop the huge man in front of him, but he could at least appeal to his common sense.

"Look, you got these kids here safe. You can't just abandon them."

Jack was not to be swayed. "One of their teachers is in there – Owen Beavin. He said he'll look after them. They're in safe hands."

"That's as maybe," the Warden continued, "But one of them boys is your own son, I understand. How would he feel if you ran out there and got killed? The incendiaries have stopped for now but there'll be real bombs following. You can't kick one of those across the road."

Jack looked at him. Evidently he had seen Geraint's act too and blamed him for the boy's recklessness.

"The rest of my family are out there too," he said, looking the man in the eye. "I need to know they're safe."

Gladys and little Marie would have been at home in Tan Y Marian Street when the attack started, and if that was the case Jack had to hope that they had gone across the road to the Coslett's, as planned, and used their Anderson shelter. There had been a couple of smaller bombing raids a few weeks before and the four of them, plus his mother, had all joined the Coslett's in relative safety. It was crowded but better than the alternative.

His other daughters, Eileen, Helen and Lilley, all had shelters of their own, either in their gardens or, in Eileen's case, via a public shelter in the next street. They and their families should be safe. Winifred was thankfully far away from the danger in Glasgow, where her husband of 5 years lived. Jack still hadn't warmed to George Blockley, but he had to accept that at least he'd made sure one daughter would be safe on this hellish night.

Everything told him that his family should be safe but still he had to go and find them for himself. He couldn't forgive himself if something happened and he wasn't there.

The Warden could see there was no arguing with him. "Well, look," he said, "We have to hope that their main targets will be the docks and the railway. Possibly the oil refinery too. If you can stay away from those areas, you might have a chance."

Jack nodded. Then he shook the man's hand and left the shelter.

***

The scene before him was like something out of a nightmare.

The walls of familiar buildings were lit up by the flickering of flames all around, the pitting and damage done to them transforming them into weird new shapes. The night sky glowed an eerie red as rumblings, sometimes felt more than heard, were testament to buildings collapsing in nearby streets. The pounding of the AA guns was constant and now there was a new sound to add to the mix – the whining scream of bombs falling to earth.

Jack had attempted to continue down the Strand to make his way home, but the way ahead was blocked. A building was burning, the rubble from it stretching across the street. A handful of Auxiliary Firemen, fearfully checking around them for more damage, were setting up a pump in the street to start to control it.

Jack moved on, cutting down the side of Swansea Castle, already a ruin but so far miraculously untouched by the attack, so that he could get to Oxford Street. Every other step faltered as another explosion rocked the area or he was forced to flatten himself to a wall or the ground. And yet, despite the destruction around him, despite the noise, he was struck by how empty the city seemed. Everyone safely in shelters, just fools like him on the streets.

This war was different to the one he had fought in before. Then, he had sought out battle, putting his own life and that of his fellow crewmen in danger only when they needed to. He fought at sea for the safety of his family at home. Now War had no respect for civilians or families. It came to everyone, borne on wings from distant countries and raining down fire indiscriminately. There was no safe place.

Oxford Street was surprisingly untouched by most of the carnage and, although still careful, Jack was able to make his way down it and to the crossroads with relative ease. As he turned into Union Street, however, it was a different story altogether.

Halfway down, he could see the Market - and it was on fire. Even from a distance, Jack could see that the great glass and iron roof of the Victorian building was gone. The walls seemed to be standing but flames licked at the sky from within the structure and twisted metal struts clawed at the sky like gnarled fingers.

A crowd of people were standing outside the huge arched entrance. Jack could see Wardens and more Auxiliary Firemen and Fire Watchers, plus an actual fire engine and crew. Two policemen were trying to arrange a line of people to pass buckets of water in through the arch where more men were trying to douse the nearest flames.

One of the policemen saw Jack and beckoned him over. For a second, Jack considered not going, but he knew that he couldn't do that.

"Do you know anything about pump engines?" the policeman shouted over the sound of the fire.

Jack shook his head.

"Bloody thing's not working," the policeman said, looking over to where a group of men were crowded around a small trailer. Jack recognised it as one of the Auxiliary Fire Service's Fire Pumps, an engine-driven water pump on the back of a two-wheeled trailer. He'd seen them being hauled around town behind taxis or private cars. They were designed to be used on single incendiary bombs, so he couldn't think it would be a lot of use here on its own – but with the fire brigade aiming high and this aiming at the base of the fire, it might prove useful.

At least, it would if it was working.

Jack was about to continue on when he spotted something else. He grabbed the policeman's shoulder and pointed. "What about that?"

The policeman looked to where he was pointing. Attached to another trailer, but seemingly abandoned in the street, was a similar device, but this one was rounder and had two huge handles, one sticking up from either side of it. A hand pump.

"It was first here," the policeman said. "Belongs to the street's Fire Watchers, but it's seized up. We just can't get it working. Three men tried."

"Give me a minute," Jack said as he sprinted over to the machine. The policeman shook his head and returned to his duties. Jack picked up the front of the trailer and wheeled it over to where the queue of men were throwing water onto the fire.

The heat here was so intense that, for a moment, Jack was transported back to the depths of *HMS Lion*. Another time, another war. Noise and heat and blood pounding in his ears. The air he breathed burning his throat. Men shouting and engines hammering, thumping, pummelling his senses like the distant sound of guns...

Jack felt a hand on his shoulder and he was suddenly dragged back to the present.

"It doesn't work," a young man in the AFS uniform was saying. He waved his hands in front of Jack to signify it was broken.

Jack shook his head, as much to clear the unwanted memory as to reply to the man. "Just aim the hose at the fire," he said. "Get the buckets on this side."

Although he had no reason to trust him, the young man did what Jack said, diverting the flow of buckets around to the suction hose on the other side of the pump.

As soon as everyone was in place, Jack reached up and grabbed the handle for the pump. The metal was cool to his touch but unyielding. The bar that he was pushing down on was level with his shoulders, and the force he was using was so much that the whole trailer was starting to dip towards him before the handle had moved. The young AFS man saw what was happening and rushed around to the other side of the pump, anchoring it by sitting on the edge of it.

Still the handle did not move. Jack pushed down harder, straining in the heat. He was sweating hard and was dimly aware that the back of his shirt was cold and wet where it was facing away from the heat of the fire. He continued to push, hoping the machine would give out before the handle broke, before he broke.

"It's no good –" the young man started to say. And then Jack felt something give and the handle started to swing downwards. It was hard going but the movement was smooth and fluid. As it reached the bottom of its arc, Jack lifted it back up again and felt the pull as the pump sucked water in from the bucket at its side. The young AFS man just stared at him in awe.

After that, things were a little smoother. Not easy by any count – operating the pump should have been a two-man job and it was still a little reluctant to move on the upswings – but everyone got into a rhythm and the flow of water onto the fire could now be directed to best effect. At some point, two men turned up with a tin bathtub full of water (having raided a local ironmonger whose windows had been blown out) and that gave everyone – but Jack – a short respite.

He manned the pump for just under an hour. By the end of it, Jack's shoulders felt like they were on fire and he had cramps in his stomach. He ached everywhere but despite his best efforts and those of the men around him, the fire didn't look any smaller. Eventually, even he had to stop. Two burly men took over his place on the pump. The young AFS man stepped forward and half-guided, half-supported Jack to a kerb on the opposite side of the road. Away from the fire, the big man immediately began to shiver in the February night air.

The AFS man stepped away briefly and returned with a blanket. It was crocheted and covered in a pattern of bright flowers. He draped it over Jack's shoulders.

"Sorry, it's all I could find," he said. He glanced over at the fire and seemed to decide he wasn't needed for a moment. He sat by Jack on the pavement. "That was amazing," he continued. "I know it doesn't look like we did much, but it would be a lot worse without your help. We stopped the fire spreading. You should be proud."

Jack looked at him. He seemed very young. His face was streaked with grime and soot and there were small burnt patches on his clothes.

"I saw you on stage once," the man continued. "Promoting your fairground show, stripped to the waist. You were in a Variety show with some acrobats. In Cardiff." Jack couldn't recall this particular show, but he had done lots of promotional appearances before the War, often travelling ahead of the rest of the fair to reach a venue early. "I never came to see your Whirl of Death. Mum wouldn't let me. Said it would be too upsetting for someone with my delicate sensibilities." He laughed slightly, mirthlessly. "Wonder what she'd say if she could see me now?"

The man stood up. "Category C, in case you were wondering. Not fit for the army, suitable for Home Service only. Because this is safer than fighting abroad!" He tipped an imaginary hat. "It was good to finally meet you. You lived up to your legend."

And with that, the young man turned and went back to the horrors on the other side of the street.

\*\*\*

Jack didn't know how long he sat on the kerb side. Dimly, he remembered more explosions. He watched in a detached way as a building further down from him crumpled and fell in on itself. Fire engines and police cars came and went. At some point, someone brought him some water, but it felt thick in his throat. The skin on his face was taught and sore.

A nurse appeared by his side. She spoke soothing words to him but Jack failed to take them in. She said something about burns and hospital and he allowed himself to be guided towards an ambulance. When he got there, it was full – people laid out on stretchers, packed close in together, others standing at the sides, bandaged or bleeding. Jack stopped at the door and shook his head. He muttered something about catching the next one and turned away. The nurse went to stop him, but there was another explosion nearby and she ran in that direction instead.

Jack returned to his kerb and sat down. He knew he had somewhere else to go but in his exhausted and dehydrated state, he couldn't think where. He pulled his shawl further around himself and watched as a mixture of soot and embers danced in the air in front of him.

After a little while, the guns ceased firing and the shrill alien sound of the All Clear sounded. A strange peace settled over everything. The crackling noises of burning buildings suddenly sounded comforting if you didn't know their source. A full moon could just be glimpsed through the thick smoke in the air.

Finally, another ambulance arrived. This one had room in it and Jack allowed himself to be taken off to hospital.

It was there, the following morning, that Gladys found him.

Jack had never been so happy to see anyone in all his life. He opened his arms as wide as the valleys and pulled her in to him, holding his wife until the memory of the night before receded, replaced by a love he rarely spoke aloud but felt keenly every day.

Together, strong again, they set off for home.

The Whirl of Death

## Chapter Eight

**July 1948**


It's been a while since I've been to a fair, Winnie thought

Except that wasn't true, she reflected. As the wife of a showman for 12 years, she had been to plenty of fairs – helping George to set up the great Helter Skelter or standing for hours at the booth collecting money from excited children. However, the demands of looking after their own six children had kept her away from fairgrounds for a while, especially distant ones, and on the few occasions that George had been operating nearby, she had always had the whole family in tow. But this visit was different.

Here, she was on home ground, and the children were with George for the day (although she acknowledged that the two oldest boys, Jack and George Jnr, would probably be doing most of the childcare). Here, she could relax a little and look around – and concentrate on her main reason for being there: seeing her father.

Although, she had to admit, there were aspects of their reunion she was not looking forward to.

Glasgow Green stretched out in front of her as she left its railway station. When she had first arrived in Glasgow, this had been one of her favourite places, a huge swathe of green by the side of the Clyde. It was true that you could see mountains – Bens, she corrected herself – from most places in the city, but it still didn't feel like Swansea did. The Green had helped with that.

Opposite her was the imposing entrance to the People's Palace, newly designated as a museum for the history of the city. Behind it, the huge glass conservatory twinkled in the sunlight. To her left was the Templeton Carpet Factory, it's grand and colourful façade (modelled on the Doge's Palace in Venice, she had been told) impressing even more than the museum. Aside from these buildings, and the towering monument to Admiral Nelson on her right, there was nothing but parkland, punctuated by artfully placed thickets of bushes or trees.

Even if Winnie had been unsure of where to go next, though, the crowds of people flowing out of the station with her or marching up the Green from the Saltmarket would have provided a clue. The fair was based at the Flesher Haugh ground, at the eastern end of the park, and it felt as if the whole of Glasgow was heading there.

For this was Fair Fortnight, the annual holiday for the city. Even now, five days into it, the masses of people heading for the top of the Green were hard to believe. The shipyards, the factories and all businesses were closed for two weeks, and the fair was just one of the excuses people had to party.

Many Glaswegians had already set off 'doon the watter', taking one of a fleet of steamers down river to the beaches along the coast. Places like Ayr, Largs, Troon, Rothesay, and Saltcoats found their populations suddenly swelling to breaking point as thousands of Weegies descended upon them, eager to get their 'taps aff' in the sunshine. Those who could afford it even went as far as the exotic delights of Blackpool.

On her way in that morning, Winnie had seen queues of what must have been at least a thousand people outside Central Station as they tried to get the train to Wemyss Bay. It was staggering to see how many people could leave the city at the same time – and yet it still didn't feel empty.

Partly this was because not everyone could afford a week's holiday or to leave the city every day, but it was also because the fair was an attraction in itself, drawing people in from towns outside the city like Barrhead and Hamilton. Even a Welsh import like Winnie could pick out different regional accents on the train up to Glasgow Green, a sure sign that word of the fair had travelled far.

It was, as both her husband and her father had said many times, the oldest fair in Scotland – and one of the most profitable if played right. There was the attraction of the booths and the rides, of course, but there was also a huge market attached – the real Fair, if you traced it back far enough – and that meant that people came with a mind to spend. Edinburgh could keep its new-fangled Festival – this was Glasgow's crowning glory, and it would no doubt outlast the capital's arty celebration as it had most things.

The fair itself was huge. As she came up to the gates into Flesher Haugh, Winnie marvelled at the variety on display. Normally, George's Helter Skelter would tower over most of the booths but here it was only just visible. For a start, the fronts of booths had got bigger over the years, vying for attention with gaudy colours and giant lettering promising great feats within. The tents behind them seemed small in comparison. But there was also a big wheel, and a new ride called a Dive Bomber. Or at least it looked new - Winnie realised that it was actually just a renamed Loop-o-Plane where two cars swung in opposite arcs from each other until they eventually performed a full loop. The ride looked scary, which was usually a great draw, but no one seemed keen to go on it. Perhaps it's the name, Winnie thought – it was topical, but the scars of the war were still fresh for many people.

Further over, she could see cakewalks and Halls of Mirrors and shooting booths and – yes! – her favourite ride, the Octopus! She may have been 35 years old, but seeing that took her back to childhood visits to fairs with both her parents. Just by the side of the Octopus was a Hook-A-Duck stall. Winnie smiled wryly at the game – a few years earlier, her husband had invented a new game, calling it Paddy's Pigs and asking children to hook a wooden pig's curly tail to win a prize. It had been a success and so, of course, it had been copied by other Showmen, just swapping the pigs out for some floating ducks. She'd even heard that it was now referred to as a Swanny, cementing it firmly in Showman's patter.

It was only 10 in the morning, but the grounds were already bustling. Somewhat surprisingly, there were quite a few drunken punters around too. Winnie wondered if they'd started early or were just finishing the previous night's holiday celebrations. It wasn't even as if alcohol was that easy to come by – it might not be rationed like so many other things still were, but sugar and grain were, so brewers produced far less liquor than they used to. Not that I've ever known anything come between a Glaswegian and his pint, Winnie thought with a smile. As if on cue, one man staggered up and winked at her in an exaggerated fashion. As a woman on her own, Winnie knew she was considered fair game for idiots like him, but she also knew that if he tried anything more than a wink, he'd regret it. Luckily for the man, Winnie's disinterest proved enough to sway his attentions and he staggered away towards a booth promising belly dancers instead.

Winnie knew that her father's booth was situated on the left-hand side of the field, close to the Big Wheel. It was a good spot – the wheel was a focal point, something that people could arrange to meet at, and a position next to it meant there were a lot of punters waiting around with time to kill. The Big Wheel was one of the most popular rides on the fair – stately enough to entice the nervous but with a touch of danger at its highest point that allowed men to pull their dates in close without fear of reprisal. However, despite not being a noisy ride in itself, it attracted a noisy crowd - meaning that Jack's exterior show had to be very good indeed.

Luckily, it was. There had been posters outside the railway station, plastered onto wooden boards and tied to railings, for a few attractions at the fair, but to Winnie's eyes, her father's posters were the most eye-catching. Most of the writing on them was in red with a red border around them to draw the eye. There were no pictures, but the words JACK LEMM and WHIRL OF DEATH jumped out at the reader, with a promise that the strongman would appear at every performance performing 'Feats Of Sensational Strength With Huge Weights'. Below that were the names of other acts appearing at the booth – The Phillp Sisters ('The Clever Lady Acrobats') and Jacky Lewis and Bobby Taylor, two strongmen who also helped out with the boxing side of things. The poster ended with a rousing call to SEE FREE DEMONSTRATIONS ON THE EXTERIOR before proclaiming the whole act as 'Featuring The Greatest Array of Talent Ever Produced On A Fair Ground'.

All of this, alongside the legends written large across the front of his booth – THE FAMOUS JACK LEMM STAR OF MUSIC HALL, THE STRONGEST MAN IN THE UK, THE SHOW SUPREME – and some slightly-romanticised paintings of a younger Jack, helped to draw the punters in. Some of the other booths around him presented one act, one spectacular event, and then threw the audience out, most of their extra material having been used up on the exterior show. Winnie wasn't sure if it was his Music Hall origins or just a sense of Getting Your Money's Worth, but Jack had always prized himself on presenting a full show, inside and out.

To this end, not only did he present his own strongman feats and a few physique poses on the exterior, but Jack gave equal time to the rest of his troupe. The sisters performed balancing acts first, providing a touch of femininity to draw the male punters in. Then they were joined by the two other strongmen who would lift them with one hand or toss the girls between them like human juggling sticks. It was a crowd-pleasing performance for certain, and it convinced a lot of people to part with their money for the rest of the show. Once inside the tent, the paying audience would see more acrobatics from the girls and the boys would test their ability to lift heavy weights against members of the crowd. Eventually, this would lead up to one weight that was too heavy for the two strongmen combined – and at this point, Jack would enter, hauling the huge barbell above his head as if it were no more than a small child.

After such a memorable entrance, Jack would perform a variation on his tried-and-trusted Hercules Unchained act, with members of the audience first testing the strength of the chains, and then it was on to the main attraction, The Whirl Of Death.

This was not the end of the show, however. All the performances took place on a raised platform in the middle of the tent. Partly this was to provide a theatre-in-the-round type of experience and partly it was because, with the addition of some props quickly fastened into holes in the stage, it could become a boxing ring. Whilst it was being set up, Jack would encourage anyone of a nervous disposition to leave the tent (no one ever did), and then he would open the ring up to challengers, either for himself or (depending on how tired he was) for Jacky Lewis or Bobby Taylor. Indeed, this section of the show was the main reason for the two lads being there. The Boxing Booth was a good gateway to proving yourself for professional boxing and to the lads the Strongman routine was just a sidenote. Jack was known for his coaching skills and for spotting talent like Kaiser Bates, who had gone on to be professional, so it was a mutually beneficial situation.

In total, the whole show lasted between 20-25 minutes and, during this last section, the Phillps Sisters would already be outside, usually with at least one of the boys or Jack, drumming up custom for the next performance. If the audience in the tent had enjoyed the show, and they usually did, they would toss coins into the ring before leaving and it would be the task of the troupe member running the boxing to collect this 'nobbins' and store it away for divvying up later.

Between 10am and midnight, the troupe would put on around 40 performances every day. It was a world that Winnie was all too familiar with and, if she was honest with herself, that she missed. Her own days of boxing had been tough but fun, and, despite the punishing schedule, the sense of family that the troupe had was something unequalled in her life since. But it was a young person's game. The Phillps Sisters were in their early twenties; Bobby Taylor was still only 19. Most of the showmen she knew had taken a backseat in their fifties, still running the booth but letting family or younger employees take the literal heavy lifting. Jack had turned 60 that year and he was still building the booth and travelling around in his bus, let alone taking punches every night. Her father was the strongest man she had ever known – physically and otherwise – but she worried that he might be over-taxing himself now. If he was, she knew that she would have to say something. No matter how good the intentions, however, it would not be an easy conversation.

Winnie arrived at the booth in time to see the end of Jack's exterior performance. Mostly, this comprised of him lifting an anvil placed conspicuously on the side of the stage and then hammering a 6-inch nail into a piece of wood with his bare palm - always an impressive sight. After this, Jack mainly had to show off his muscles in a variety of poses and the punters would eagerly queue to pay their entrance fee. Typically during this period, Jack didn't look out at the audience, knowing that catching someone's eye now might mean they'd become a belligerent opponent in the ring later, but all the same, he did spot Winnie and gave her a quick wink of acknowledgement.

Winnie smiled back. Her father certainly still looked an impressive man. He had lost none of his height, towering over anyone else on the stage, and the muscles of his upper body were still clearly sculpted. His torso was bare and Winnie could see the scar on his left arm, twisted in amongst the veins, his skin an almost alabaster white. Cauliflower ears and a thickening of the skin over his eyebrows, the legacy of scar tissue from fights and rugby, meant that his face was more 'characterful' than handsome, but it all added to the image of the strongman. To top it off, Jack wore a pair of blue velvet trunks edged with gold tassels, and white leggings. A weight belt was cunningly concealed in the waist of the trunks, and gladiator boots and leather wrist bands completed the outfit.

The only part of her father that really betrayed his age was his face. His hair was thinner than Winnie remembered and the skin on one side of his face seemed slightly tauter than the other, a consequence of his actions in the Swansea Blitz. His eyes glinted with a youthful vigour but still betrayed the long days and frequent travelling that was the showman's life. He stared out over the crowd like a statue, guarding and guiding in equal measures. It was an impressive sight, but Winnie knew that some of that impassive stare also came from the fact that his hearing had grown worse over the years and Jack could no longer make out individual voices in the crowd.

Winnie looked at the queue and decided to nip around the side of the booth to the back of the tent. As expected, Jacky Lewis was there, making sure no one tried to sneak in without paying. He was sat on an upturned bucket, a half-eaten carrot in one hand.

"Bloody hell," Winnie smiled. "It's Oor Wullie!"

The reference escaped Jacky, but he smiled anyway. The two had met before, albeit some time ago, and he remembered the boss' daughter.

"In to see the show?" he asked.

Winnie liked Jacky. He was slow to anger and provided a good, grounded presence for the rest of the troupe. Without him, many an argument could easily have run out of control. She wondered if she should ask him to be around later, depending upon what she saw in the tent, then dismissed it.

Any conversation should just be between father and daughter.

"If that's okay with you," she said. In reply, Jacky took another crunch out of his carrot, then stood up and pulled a tent flap open. He made an exaggerated bow as he did so. Winnie mock-curtsied and slipped in through the gap.

Inside the tent was dark and it took a few moments for her eyes to become accustomed to it. There were lights, hanging over and around the stage, but not all of them were on, allowing the daylight filtering through the striped tent walls to do the hard work. Although it was still only the start of the day, the air smelled of stale sweat and cigarette smoke. Some of the punters wrinkled their noses as they came in, but, to Winnie, it was a comforting, familiar smell. There were no seats - partly because they were just another thing to haul from place to place in a truck with limited space and partly because they could become weapons if the boxing portion of the show turned nasty – so Winnie took her place by one of the tent walls. She knew that she'd have a good view there and the rest of the audience would crowd up to the stage, so she'd also be relatively free from any unwanted attention.

The show began and for the first ten minutes Winnie concentrated on watching the audience. At this time of day, everyone was quite well behaved. Tonight's rowdy drunks were still seeking out their next 'hauf an a hauf' (a whisky and a half pint of beer) and young men out to impress their girls were still trying to convince their parents to let them go to the fair on their own. This audience was mainly family men, husbands and wives, some teenage children. The applause was sluggish but the desire to be entertained was still there.

Even the most jaded audience member perked up, however, when Jack's weightlifting act was cut short by the sound of an angry engine. Everyone turned to see a motorbike with the two Phillps sisters sat on it, revving in the doorway into the tent. The crowd parted as it made its way to the stage and a ramp that led up to it. This, they knew, was the main attraction – The Whirl of Death.

Whilst everyone had been distracted, Jack had moved his weights to the furthest edges of the stage. Now he stood dead centre as the motorbike and riders approached him.

If anyone had looked at the motorcycle closely, they might have noticed a few unusual things about it. For a start, it was an 'Indian' motorcycle, a bike made by the Hendee Motorcycle Company of Springfield, Massachusetts. Jack had owned this bike since his Wall Of Death days, where it was frequently the vehicle of choice given its deliberately low centre of gravity and low-slung handlebars. It made the same noise as a standard motorcycle, especially inside the tent, but it was slightly lighter and, handily for what was to come, had all its controls on the left-hand side.

The bike began a slow anti-clockwise prowl around Jack on the stage. He turned with it, so that he was always facing the machine. Watching him, Winnie could see how his steps were falling into a rhythm, allowing him to turn without tripping as the bike started to speed up. The audience were entranced but Winnie doubted any of them realised what was really happening. Their attention was on the driver; Jack's was on the pillion passenger.

Winnie saw him give a barely visible nod and the Phillps sister on the back of the bike suddenly leapt off it and onto his shoulders. Quickly, she looped a leather strap around the back of Jack's neck and then swung herself around him to hang off his back. The loss of the passenger's weight on the bike meant that it sped up suddenly and Jack, briefly matching it in speed, lifted the machine up off the ground by the strap. The sister who was driving put her head down and flattened herself along the body of the bike as much as she could. At the same time, Jack reached out and grabbed the handlebars and the back of the pillion seat to steady it (and to take some pressure off his neck) and then continued to spin around with both the girls and the bike swinging out at an angle away from him.

The audience cheered. The speed of the move had dazzled them and now they realised what they were watching – a dangerous feat of strength. Winnie knew the dangers better than any of them. When she was younger and lighter, she had been the pillion passenger for this act with her elder sister Lily driving. To mis-time it was to risk serious injury for Jack, for both bike riders and for the audience. For the briefest of moments, until the pillion passenger could counterbalance it, Jack's neck was taking all the burden – and he wasn't even able to stand still and plant himself to take the strain. Furthermore, if he fell out of rhythm with the bike or felt dizzy at any point, he could risk tearing his shoulders or his knees and once again endangering everyone there. It was an incredible act, and as always, her father made it look easy.

Jack did not hold the pose for long. Two circuits of the audience were enough for everyone to see it and still want more. Winnie looked on as another dangerous part of the act approached.

With the controls on his side of the handlebar, Jack squeezed the throttle on the bike as he started to lower it to the floor again. This had the dual effect of making the audience look up in fright and alerting the two sisters to the next move. As the wheels of the bike touched the stage and gained purchase, the sister on Jack's back snapped a catch on the back of the strap around his neck and the machine was freed. Jack suddenly stopped revolving and stood upright, allowing the girl to drop gracefully from his back. Meanwhile, the other sister, feeling the bike touch the ground, assessed her direction quickly and steered the machine back into its circuit of the stage. A split second wrong either way and Jack could have been pulled off balance and under the wheels of the bike – or it could have careened off the stage into the audience. Neither of these things happened.

The motorbike pulled up at the start of the ramp and the audience went wild. Winnie realised that she had been holding her breath and exhaled thankfully.

The two Phillps Sisters re-joined Jack on stage and took their bows. As her father started in on his patter for the Boxing matches, Winnie slipped out through the exit to the front of the booth.

Once more in the sunshine, Winnie was able to think about what she'd just seen. It was strange being back with her father's show but not being part of it. Yet this new outsider's point of view also allowed her to assess it calmly. She'd come here wondering if her father was still up to the rigours of the showman's life and, a few wrinkles and thinning hair notwithstanding, she had to admit that he was. Jack at 60 easily had the fortitude of men twenty years his junior. Hell, he probably had more strength and vigour than her husband!

Winnie was smiling at this thought as her father joined her.

Jack wrapped her in a big warm hug. She could smell the sweat on him and the faint chalky aroma of the powder he put on his hands to grip better. He guided her to the side of the booth where they could talk unseen.

"So good to see you," he said. "I was hoping you would get time to come over. Where are all my beautiful grandchildren?"

Winnie explained how she was free for the day and watched as her father scowled slightly at the name of her husband. That was an old argument, though. If the two wanted to speak, they were sharing a ground for the next week, let them do it – but Winnie knew they had worked the same fairs before, and Jack had never sought out his son-in-law. It was too much effort to bring it up again, so she changed the subject.

"The show was good," she said. Without realising it, she was speaking louder than she normally would have to accommodate Jack's deafness.

Jack glanced at her, then looked down at the ground.

"I nearly dropped the bike," he said. "At the end, when I was putting her down. My hand slipped, just a bit."

"Which hand?" Winnie asked, but she knew the answer already.

"The left," Jack said. The last time she'd seen him, he'd been flexing that arm a lot, squeezing on a hard rubber ball whenever he got the chance. Arthritis.

"I'm teaching Jacky how to do the Whirl," he continued. "Just in case. I'll still run it – he won't be able to take it anywhere else – but I can take the odd day off."

Winnie was relieved to hear him say it. "You'll have to change the posters."

Her father smiled. "Jack Lemm Presents..." he said, marking out the shape of an arc in the air with his hands.

Winnie smiled back. "Does this mean Mum will get to see more of you in the future?"

"I hope so. Not immediately, and don't you tell her about this – I don't want her nagging about my arm. Or about when I'm coming home. But it's part of the plan, yes."

Winnie looked at him. It was probably the nearest she would ever get to hearing her father proclaim his love, but in his terms, this was shouting it from the rooftops.

One of the Sisters popped her head around the side. "Sorry, Jack," she said. "Not many people interested in boxing at this time of day. We're nearly done here."

Jack nodded and indicated that he'd be there in a minute.

"Duty calls," he said, pulling Winnie in to him for another hug. "I hope you'll call this way again before we move on. Maybe bring some of those kids of yours. John must be old enough to box by now."

Father and daughter parted, him back to the business of drawing a crowd, her fading away into one. Winnie looked back at the booth and her father calling out to passers-by to gain their attention. He was made for this, she thought.

Then she set her sights on the Helter Skelter in the distance and went off to find her own family.

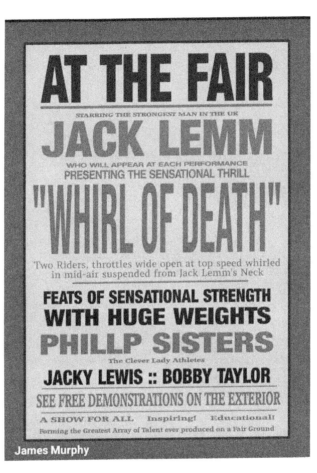

A facsimile of one of Jack's posters

(James Murphy)

## Chapter Nine

### June 2nd, 1953

"I said I'd bring you to London one day," Jack said, his eyes twinkling.

Gladys looked around her. There was a steady drizzle of rain in the air and the ground underfoot was soggy and starting to turn to mud after many heavy boots had walked across it. Across the road from them, the town of Woolwich was just emerging from a heavy smog.

"Not exactly paved with gold, is it?" she said, but there was a smile with her words.

"Ah, come on now, girl," her husband replied. "You wouldn't want to be in the middle of all those crowds in the city, anyway, would you?"

To be honest, Gladys probably wouldn't have minded. She had never been to London before (and, apparently, wasn't going to see the city this time either), and crowds had never been a problem for her. Plus, how many Coronations was she likely to see in her lifetime?

But, on the other hand, she was at least closer to the event than she would be in Swansea, and the whole town – the whole *country*! - had come out to celebrate, so the atmosphere was probably just as good as on the Mall.

In the meantime, she was getting to spend some time with her husband, and he'd even taken a little time off from the booth to walk the fairground with her. Gladys was pleased by this turn of events, but it slightly worried her as well. She could see that there was something on Jack's mind, had noticed it as soon as she'd arrived, and until she found out what it was, she would still be a little on edge.

The Fair on Woolwich Common had been the idea of Henry Botton, a local showman who ran this particular ground. He'd wanted a fair to celebrate the crowning of the new Queen, but he wanted to make it something special in showman's terms as well. To that end, he'd invited the Codona's down from Scotland, and a few Welsh families as well, to create a United Kingdom Coronation Fair (it was considered too difficult for Irish showmen to get their rides and booths over for just a week, but there were enough Irishmen working on the rides anyway that it helped to fill out the idea).

To further boost the occasion, the fair had been opened with a Civic Ceremony on the Saturday, four days earlier. With great pomp, the Mayor of Woolwich had grandly cut a ribbon on the steps of the StratoRocket before, less grandly, sliding down the Helter Skelter for the press. The Chairman of the Showman's Guild and a few other dignitaries present evidently didn't feel the need for the extra publicity and kept their feet firmly on the ground.

Botton had arranged an Ox Roast for the day itself (having gained special permission from the Ministry of Food, as meat was still rationed to 2 shillings per week) and there was to be a fireworks display to close the proceedings. Union jacks flew from the tops of booths and red, white and blue blunting – last hoisted for VE Day - adorned most rides. Most of the booths that dished out prizes, like the shooting stalls or the ball games, had swapped their cuddly toys for Coronation souvenirs (with the hope that they would get through them before the week ended) and the crowds arrived in their hundreds. Everywhere there was the typical British spirit of people enjoying themselves despite the weather.

Jack had been invited down by the Codona's themselves and his booth was amongst their rides rather than those from Wales. The Scottish Showmen had endured a long and arduous journey coming down from Aberdeen. Each day had been a 15-18 hour drive, manoeuvring their great trailers and caravans through small towns and congested cities alike. Never managing to get above 22 miles per hour (and averaging considerably less), the 500-mile trip was a labour of love. Even stopping off to take part in the Wanstead Flats Whitsun Bank Holiday Fair on the way – where Jack joined them – wouldn't help to cover the costs of the journey. They did it because they wanted to be part of this day – and because they wanted to show off what Scottish showmen were capable of.

Jack joked that he was now an honorary Scot, but his Welsh accent still marked him out from the other barkers around him. Even so, his position next to Gordon Codona's Waltzer was a prime spot. The Waltzer, despite having been hell to transport, was a novelty in the South and a great crowd puller. It was especially popular with young couples seeking some time alone - and, after your girl had clung to you in mock terror for ten minutes, where better to go than a boxing booth, where you could (hopefully) exhibit even more manly prowess in the ring? It was a marriage made in Showman Heaven. Okay, sometimes Jack had to strain to be heard over the Waltzer's speakers blaring out a recording of Winifred Atwell's honky-tonk piano hit 'Coronation Rag', but on the whole it wasn't a problem. At least he wasn't competing with the crooning of Frankie Laine and that ruddy dirge 'I Believe' which seemed to be playing everywhere else.

Gladys glanced over to a clock on a nearby darts stall. It was only 11:30am. Still around a half hour before the Coronation was to begin. She had plenty of time to get to the StratoRocket by then.

"You alright, girl?" Jack asked.

Gladys smiled and nodded. She still wasn't used to having him nearby so much and his constant concern for her was feeding into her paranoia over what he was keeping from her. Jack had been at home with her and the family during the war, but outside of that she'd seen very little of him. A network of charter fairs and town fairs throughout Wales gave him business enough, taking Jack from Abergavenny to Neath or Caerphilly to Wrexham in a criss-crossing pattern of touring routes. Beyond that there were the big fairs of England – St Giles' Fair in Oxford, the Goose Fair in Nottingham, Newcastle Town Moor Fair, the Sefton Park Liverpool fair, Scarborough, Hull... the list went on. Occasionally, Gladys had been able to join him at a fairground, but it was more likely for her to be at home, getting the odd phone call or the even-more infrequent letter. She was aware the two of them inhabited different worlds for most of the time, and that they only occasionally overlapped, so times like this were precious.

Even so, Gladys had become a strong-minded and independent woman over those years without him. She had brought up eight children with just the help of her mother-in-law, and lost five others either at birth or through illness shortly thereafter. Jack had not always been there for those times or their aftermath, no matter how much he had wanted to be, and pain and loss had hardened Gladys more than she thought he realised. To have him now looking out for her was both comforting and slightly aggravating and right now she wasn't sure which side would win out.

These were thoughts for another day, though, she admonished herself. Jack was making a real effort to be with her, and she enjoyed the company of the Codonas and the other showmen families, most of whom she knew at least faintly. Enjoy the moment, she decided.

A cheery voice broke into her thoughts. "Is this Winnie's younger sister, then?"

Gladys had to think about the question for a moment, given the strong Glaswegian accent that it was wrapped in. She looked over to see Jimmy

Thomas smiling at her. She liked Jimmy – his face never seemed to be far away from a wink and, as his question suggested, he was friends with her daughter, Winnie. He lived with his wife and son, out of season, on the winter grounds in Moorhouse in the east end of Glasgow and her daughter had spoken of visiting the area many times.

"Unless Winnie is looking particularly bad these days, you'll know that I'm her mother," Gladys said back, but all the same she was secretly pleased with the compliment.

Jimmy was at the fair with his Jolly Tubes, three huge rotating cylinders on the back of a truck. Punters tried to stay upright in them as they turned, the centre cylinder going the opposite way to the two outer ones. It was a popular attraction and Jimmy had gone all out with patriotic flags covering the exterior. Unfortunately, this was slightly at odds with the huge sign above it proclaiming the attraction as 'The New American Comedy Ride'.

"But then perhaps I shouldn't trust your eyesight anyway if you can't tell the difference between a Union Jack and the Stars and Stripes," Gladys continued.

Jimmy laughed. "The punters don't seem to care. They're loving it. Care to give it a try?"

"At 60?" Gladys exclaimed. "I've difficulty enough walking on this turf, let alone your contraption. Thank you, but no."

Jimmy winked at her. "Your loss." He turned to Jack and started to talk to him about the journey down and Gladys stepped away from the two of them to let them natter.

Gladys glanced over to the StratoRocket. It was the centrepiece of the Scottish section of the fair and easily visible from anywhere on the grounds. Steps at the front led to the circular rocket cars within. These spun on their own axis whilst also being carried on a track in a clockwise direction. A central dome spun counterclockwise, giving the effect to any passengers that they were going a lot faster than they were. It was one of the largest standard machines to travel in the country and had never been this far South before, having been transported to Woolwich by 3 Leyland lorries, each pulling another truck or living wagon behind them. The dark crimson, gold and red livery of the ride stood out even in the grey drizzle and the sounds of excited screams could be heard coming from it all day.

However, it was what was behind the StratoRocket that concerned Gladys the most.

The Codona family had set up John Codona's Pleasure Fairs Ltd in 1943 and Jack, mainly through his friendship with the eldest son William Codona, and partly because he could be depended upon, had orbited their attractions for some time. Then, only a year ago, William had suddenly and unexpectedly died at the age of 44.

He left a widow, Mary, and an 18-year old son, John. Jack had attended the funeral, as had many showmen, and had offered his assistance should the family need it. The business continued to be run by the two surviving brothers, Alfred and Gordon, but Jack's kindness had been remembered and that was part of the reasoning behind his invitation to join the Coronation Fair. Gladys had met Mary before, in happier days, and the two women had got on well. As a result, when she had found out Gladys would be there, Mary invited her over to her living wagon to watch the Coronation.

On a Television.

If anything told people that Mary was part of Showman Royalty, the fact that she had the ability to host a soirée to show off her television would be it.

Mary and John now ran the StratoRocket and, as befitted the owners of one of the great attractions, Mary had a sumptuous living wagon.

Positioned behind the ride, hidden away from the lorries and box trucks, was a handsome 30-foot Southern living wagon. The wagon couldn't be too close to the lorries as most of them were being used as shaft-drive generators for the rides and booths. This was where the Scottish showmen really impressed their English counterparts – that famous symbol of the fairground, the traction engine, was virtually gone from Scottish fairs, replaced by the heat and noise of dependable Gardner diesel engines powering the lighting and attractions via a dynamo coupled to the lorries' drive shaft.

Mary's accommodation stood out from the other wagons partly because of its size and partly through its bold paintwork, simulating a brown woodgrain with gold highlights on the windows and panels. It was by far the most impressive living accommodation at the fair and Gladys would have been desperate to see inside it even without the lure of the television. Surreptitious glances through windows festooned with cut glass images of grapes around the edges and baskets of flowers in the centre had suggested lots of crystal ware and highly polished glass within. Rumour had it there was even a sunken bath.

Gladys knew that there wouldn't be too many people at the gathering. For most of the showmen, this was just an ordinary day. They were aware of the pomp and circumstance going on in the city, but business was not going to stop for it. The punters would still be there, so the booths would stay open. It was mainly the visitors - the wives and children who weren't working - who would get the chance to see history being made in black and white on a tiny screen.

Jack and Jimmy were finishing up their conversation and shaking hands. Jimmy looked across to Gladys and gave a courteous nod before heading back to his ride.

"He was telling me there was a bit of bother at Johnny Matchett's shooting stall last night," Jack said as he joined his wife. "Some of the squaddies from the barracks were getting a bit rowdy, saying the rifles must be fixed because they'd always shot better than that on the range. Of course, when they shot there, they wouldn't have been three sheets to the wind, but they didn't think of that.  The argument got settled before it got nasty, though – Johnny's young lad scored three bullseyes to prove the guns weren't rigged." Jack laughed. "They couldn't argue after being beaten by a 10-year old!"

Gladys smiled back at him. The story wasn't that funny but she loved to see him laugh. It wasn't that Jack was a dour man, but he was sparing with his smiles. When they arrived, you felt as if they had really been earned, and if you were the reason for a smile, you felt privileged to receive it. Similarly, in keeping with the strongman's image, Jack presented a stony front to the world. Only the lucky few got to hear his laugh.

"I need to be getting over to Mary's," Gladys said. She felt a little crestfallen to see the smile fade from his face.

"Aye, I suppose I should get back to the booth as well," Jack said. "It's just…"

His words tailed off.

"What?" Gladys asked.

"I just had something I wanted to say," Jack replied.

Gladys was surprised to feel a little ripple of cold run down her back. This was the moment she had been dreading. It was unlike Jack to not speak his mind. For him to hesitate over something meant it must be something big.

Was it his health? She knew of his arthritis, and his hearing was slightly better since he'd been given the hearing aids that ex-Servicemen were entitled to (even if he didn't wear them when performing). But he wasn't a young man anymore, and his body had been through a lot, both in the wars and professionally. Surely someone could only stay strong for so long… Instinctively, she glanced down at his hands to see if there were any tremors, but there didn't seem to be. She looked up into his eyes and waited.

"I wanted to tell you this somewhere better," Jack said at last. "Somewhere drier, anyway." He gave her a faint smile.

"You know I've been pulling back from the booth a bit lately. Well, trying. Jobs just keep coming up and, well... Anyway, I've been trying. Well, the thing is, I didn't want to give anything up until I had somewhere for the troupe to go. And I've sorted out work now for Jacky and Bobby, and the sisters have found stuff for themselves, so..."

"You're coming home?" Gladys asked. This was not what she had been expecting.

Jack nodded, looking down at the grass. "If you'll have me."

Gladys stared at him. "You daft bugger!" She punched him on the arm. Jack made a show of grimacing at the action but she doubted he felt it.

"If I'll have you? Of course, I'll have you. You had me worried sick. I thought you were ill or something – you're not, are you?"

Jack shook his head. "No more than usual."

That wasn't exactly a ringing endorsement, but Gladys took it.

"Look, it won't be till the end of the summer," Jack said. "I mean, we've got commitments, and the sisters don't start until September, but I thought you might need time to prepare. For having me back, messing the place up."

Gladys took the step between them and hugged him close to her. Jack gently moved a wet strand of hair from out of her eyes and smiled down at her.

"Were you really worried?" Gladys said. "That I'd say no?"

"It crossed my mind," he said. "I mean, I know I'm your husband, but these are modern times. There's a Queen coming onto the throne, world's changing. Some wives don't want a travelling husband back. And... I've not always been there when you needed me. I know that. I don't know what good I would have been, but I know not being there meant we never got the chance to find out."

Gladys looked into his eyes. Maybe they weren't in separate worlds after all, just at different points on the same map. Still distant, but with the ability to move towards one another.

She realised how relieved she was to hear him say this. Not just that he was coming home – and adjustments would need to be made on both sides if that was to work – but that he had thought of her reaction to it. Similarly, she now thought of him.

"I know you, Jack Lamnea, you'll need to find something to take up your time when you get back too, so we'll need to find that."

"Well...," Jack grinned and she knew he was already way ahead of her on this. "I've been writing to the Invictus Club and they are looking for someone to help coach the Junior Boxers, and some of the Seniors too. Plus, I'm thinking of taking up promoting again too, if the talent is there. So I think I might be able to fill some time with that. Perhaps Teddy might even like to come back to it."

Gladys looked at him. "I think that ship has sailed," she said, and then watched a goofy smile spread across her husband's face as she realised he was pulling her leg.

The two of them jumped suddenly as a loud series of explosions filled the air. It was the artillery gun salute from the nearby Woolwich barracks – and that meant that Britain had a new monarch.

"You missed your Coronation," Jack said. He was about to apologise but Gladys put a hand to his lips.

"I'm in the best place I could be," she said, and pulled him closer in the rain.

Jack and Gladys in 1961

Jack and Gladys got another ten happy years together before Gladys died in 1963, aged 71.

Jack continued his weight training throughout this period – and beyond – and coached many young boxers, some to professional standards. Despite his age, he was a respected Physical Instructor. At the age of 70, he is remembered as going out to help some workmen dig up the road outside his house, in order to give them a break. He continued to fast one day a week to maintain his physique.

After Gladys' death, Jack's daughter Winnie, now divorced, moved to Wales to take care of him in the family home at Tan Y Marion Road, Mayhill,

Swansea. At the bottom of the garden was a corrugated green shed which he used as a gym. Even in his late 70s, his family can remember him lifting weights. They said that there were four 20kg weights on either side of a bar and that the bar would bend as he lifted it.

Outside of that, he lived a quiet and stoic life. Never one to trust banks, Jack used to collect his pension from the local Post Office and store it in his mattress. He would sit in a chair by an open fire and toast marshmallows for the younger members of his family or play the harmonica, a skill he picked up in the Navy.

Two Turkish swords hung over the fireplace.

In 1980, Giovani Lamnea Jnr – Jack Lamnea to some, Jack Lemm to more – died peacefully at the age of 92. He was buried next to his beloved Gladys.

Jack in his 80's

Two of Jack's booths over the years

A drawing of Jack's touring bus by Craig
Blockley

## Afterword – D J Thacker:

When my best friend suggested we write a book together, I couldn't have imagined the path it would take me down.

I had already written two other books – but they were Fantasy /Horror works and a very different beast to what he was suggesting. The story of his Great Grandfather Jack Lemm was certainly fascinating, but it needed research, *lots* of research, and crossed into several different worlds: Fairgrounds, Music Hall, two World Wars... It was a daunting project, and in the end it took over a year to complete.

There were challenges along the way – it didn't help that Jack changed his name several times, or that there was another strongman who overlapped with him called *John* Lemm – but in the end we found a way through all that. The key to Jack's story, we realised, was not his many accomplishments or the worlds he moved through – it was what remained constant to him. It was his family.

Naturally, this book was always going to be a fictionalised account of the life and times of Giovanni (Jack) Lamnea Jnr. In telling it, we have anchored the story in certain events and places that we know he experienced, and along the way we have introduced characters that he either met or could have met, and then embellished a little bit from there. It's been great fun finding out about everything that Jack could have experienced and talking with his surviving family, but our main goal was to tell an interesting story and to portray at least the essence of a very singular man.

I hope we did Jack proud.

Three of Jack's Grandsons - Leslie, Kenneth and Philip Lemm

**Acknowledgements**

Susan Barr (Beta Reader)

Craig Blockley (Great Grandson to Jack Lemm)

Garry Blockley (Great Grandson to Jack Lemm)

Jack Blockley (Grandson to Jack Lemm)

Irene Bowden (Granddaughter to Jack Lemm)

Cat Cochrane (Writer, poet and Beta Reader)

William Codona (Codona Family Historian)

Alan Ingram (Fairground Enthusiast, Scotland)

Leslie Lemm (Grandson to Jack Lemm)

Philip Lemm (Grandson to Jack Lemm)

Alan Mercer (Wall of Death enthusiast)

Victoria Murphy/Lemm  (Partner to Leslie Lemm)

Jim Patterson (Showman)

Cheryl Rewbridge (Great Granddaughter to Jack Lemm)

Kevin Scrivens (Fairground enthusiast and author)


**Thanks also to:**

National Fairground and Circus Archive at The University of Sheffield

The People's Collection Wales

West Sussex & The Great War Project

*A Social History of Royal Naval Stokers 1850-1950*, Tony Chamberlain, University of Exeter

World's Fair Newspaper

MyHeritage.com

Wikipedia and the great resource of the internet

## About The Author:

Steven Blockley is the fourth generation from his Great Grandfather, Jack Lemm. His Grandmother was Winnie Lemm, and his Father is George Blockley, both from Swansea.

Steven has fond memories as a kid of his Dad always trying to put a pair of brown leather boxing gloves on him. From an early age, his Dad had high hopes of Steven being a star boxer like his own Grandfather Jack Lemm. However, Steven was having none of it.

Steven, however, always had a different dream. After listening to his uncles and aunts through the years and their fascinating stories about all the incredible achievements of his Great Grandfather Jack, he wanted to write a book to bring his story to all the extended family of Jack and a wider audience.

Now his dream has finally came true. Enjoy!

## About The Author:

David J Thacker was born in 1964 and has worked in theatre for most of his life. He is the author of a novella, *The Red House* (longlisted for a British Fantasy Award), and a novel, *Once: A Belmouth Tale*. Both are available through Amazon.

He also wrote a Play for Young People (*S.O.T – Save Our Theatre*) which was performed at the Edinburgh Fringe Festival in 2001, and has penned the Libretto for a modern Oratorio, performed in 2000.

He co-wrote and directed the 2014 Retro Hugo Awards Ceremony for the 72nd World Science Fiction Convention. LonCon 3, and directed the 2014 Hugo Awards Ceremony at the same event. In 2022, he will be directing the Hugo Awards Ceremony in Chicago for the 80th World Science Fiction Convention. He lives in Glasgow.

Printed in Great Britain
by Amazon

21781082R00116